THE CROWN

FOUR FAE FOR THE PRINCESS

BOOK THREE

SADIE WATERS

For Coach Tuck, even though you threw erasers at us.

CONTENTS

THE WORLD TURNED UPSIDE DOWN

Thick smoke coils through the air, darkening the skies with its power. It burns my nostrils and lungs as I breathe in, leaving behind the unpleasant feeling of choking. My people are suffocating under its weight, and I am the only one left with the power to save them.

I look across the fields where the ground is littered with the dead, both ours and our enemy's. Blood slicks the soil in muddy rivers, soaking into the roots of this land I've inherited to lead. We are now a nation that will be built on blood and bone, if we even survive this war. It's gone on for too long.

Enough is enough.

I walk to the center of the battlefield, where soldiers have become too weak and sick to really put their hearts into the fight. My people are exhausted, starving, likely days away from death. If I do not put an end to this war, all will be lost. Altinna will have no future beyond me, and that is not a weight I am willing to bear.

Behind me, my Four wait in silence, ready to protect or attack, or silently stand in support as I do what must be done. Each of them is a piece of me. Each loves me with a burning desire that we have not yet quenched. If this is to be my last stand, I'm grateful to have them with me, ready to die or to conquer. We don't know which yet.

Ciaran is sharp-eyed and fire-veined, the warrior who'd walked into my court with a bloodstained sword and vowed to be mine. Thalen is, as always, quiet as moonlight, his magic always watching, his thoughts deeper than time itself. Roen remains unyielding and loyal, with hands that could heal or destroy, depending on his will. And my Lysen, whose laughter used to echo through my chambers like birdsong before the world began to die–I hope this will bring his laughter back.

My people say I am the First and Last Queen. In this endless war, it's been impossible to see any future for our kingdom. We are young, still, barely established. But we grew fast, posing a threat to surrounding nations. And we have access to resources they do not. Their jealousy consumed them and they banded together against us, attacking on all sides.

I am the last hope for my people. We cannot conquer with the small band of soldiers we have, who were barely ready for a fraction of this conflict. Our last hope is a barrier, magical and strong, that will protect our kingdom for generations… but only if I can get this right. Without the support of my Four, I would not have the strength to erect it on my own.

The magic inside me stirs, coiled and waiting. It knows what I must do, the enormous weight of responsibility that bears down on me. Behind me, my Four ready themselves, none of us truly sure what this spell will entail, but they've followed me to the middle of the battlefield anyway. They trust me with their whole beings, just as I trust them.

I raise my eyes to the distant hills, where the last of our enemies gather with their own sorcery. They are ready to take what scraps are left of our kingdom after they wipe us off the map. I hear the call of their horns, warning of their impending attack.

We are out of time.

If I fail, we are doomed. But I cannot let that thought deter me. I step forward, careful not to step on any of the dead. My Four place themselves in an equidistant circle around me, projecting their power and strength to me. As our enemies bear down, we commune with each other, reaching into our own depths, into the depths of the very ground, to conjure the powerful magic we need.

There is no spell for this, no stories passed down of anything like this ever happening before. We only have our hope and our trust to guide us. In a moment, it's as though I can feel the power of every dead fae who sacrificed themselves to the battle, every living fae who stands terrified of what's to come. I feel the power of my entire kingdom surge into me, and I surrender myself to the immense power of it all.

I feel my body lift off the ground, though I don't think I'm intentionally flying. It's the magic that's propelling me up and up and up. Sound explodes around me and within me, and I find it impossible to determine the external from the internal. The world is fracturing into chaos, into splintered light, into unadulterated power.

I am magic itself, my entire body vibrating, transforming into something wholly unrecognizable. There is light and pain and explosion all around me, but I'm untouched by any of it, so consumed by the power.

This must work. If my people are to survive, this barrier must hold. I concentrate on it, breathe it into existence, surrender every fiber of my being to its creation.

The world shatters below me.

Maerilee

THE PALACE HALLS ARE A BLUR OF STONE AND SHADOW AS WE RUN, THE echo of our boots crashing against the marble in a desperate rhythm. I clutch the vial of Bright Waters so tightly it makes my fingers ache.

The water sloshes dangerously in the vial, but I cannot let go of it. It's the only thing keeping me sane.

My pulse drums in my ears so hard it's the only sound I can hear. We're almost there, just a little farther to go.

The barrier to the kingdom is still holding, but barely. We were able to get through when Commander Heela and Diereken's forces could not. It's weak and frayed at the edges but still intact for now. It was one small miracle, allowing us the precious time we needed to get to Mother. Once I give her the Bright Waters, she can strengthen the barrier, and we will have more time to strategize.

Now, though, time is of the essence. My heart thrums in my chest as I push my body harder than I ever have before. We charge through the final corridor. Akin is at one side, sword drawn, ready to take down anyone who dares get in our way. River's on the other side of me, his movements fidgety and impatient. Brook and Permiton bring up the rear, a bit slower than we are. They're protected by the small band of Altinnian rebels who've come with us.

We are quite literally running for our lives, for the lives of every person who lives in this kingdom. If our enemies attack us all at once, we are done for. Mother must wake up. I cling to the hope that she will, rather than the dread that she may not.

The five of us are able to enter through the barrier I erected in Mother's chambers before we left. The rebels station themselves outside, ready to pounce on anyone who tries to stop us. I look at the pale faces of my siblings, who look equally terrified and relieved when they see us burst through the door.

"Thank the gods," Carmelina, my youngest sister exclaims, springing up to hug me.

I squeeze her quickly before releasing her, moving to where my mother lies on a chaise, her skin pale and slick with sweat. Her hair clings to her face. Her lips are dry and cracked. She already looks dead, but thankfully, I see her chest rise and fall very slowly. Father is beside her, holding her hand, his face lined with exhaustion.

"Maerilee," he says, his voice catching. "I was so afraid you wouldn't make it back."

I barely acknowledge him, too focused on what I must do. I drop to my knees beside Mother and uncork the vial in my hands. The Bright Waters shimmer like starlight as they touch her lips, and I watch as she swallows. For a breathless moment, everything stills.

Please work, please work, please work, I pray silently to myself, holding my breath.

Then, she gasps. Her chest jerks, her fingers twitch, and she blinks slowly, her eyes fluttering open.

"What's going on?" she asks weakly as she slowly takes in her surroundings. Her voice is hoarse from disuse, and she looks smaller and frailer than I've ever seen.

But she's awake. She's alive.

The Bright Waters did what they were meant to do.

My vision blurs with tears. "Mother," I sob, feeling like I can breathe for the first time in days. "You're safe now."

Her gaze moves from me to Father, then to the others.

"Oh, my darlings," she whispers, outstretching her arms so that my siblings and I can all embrace her. We squeeze her tightly, so happy that she is alive.

"You must strengthen the barrier," Permiton says carefully behind me. "We don't have much time."

Mother blinks up at him before her gaze sweeps over Akin, River, and Brook. Then her eyes scan over the doorway, where the rebels are still stationed, swords drawn.

"What's happened?" she asks.

"Eirliwyn poisoned you," I remind her. "He and Diereken were working together to overthrow you."

"I'm afraid there isn't much time, Queen Kimalissa," Akin interjects, bowing in front of her in humility and reverence. "We can explain it all later, but right now we need your magic to strengthen the barrier. The Oceanan army has teamed up with Diereken… and they're just beyond the border."

Mother nods, her face becoming serious and sharp, the way it always is when she's leading meetings. She doesn't need more details than that. Altinna is in danger and she can help. That is all that matters to her. She closes her eyes and lifts her hands, accessing her powerful magic. But then her expression changes, first to confusion and then to panic.

"No," she whispers. She lifts her hands and tries again. "No!"

I reach for her.

"What is it, Mother?" I whisper.

She doesn't answer. She throws her hands out, summoning the spell she's cast a thousand times before.

Nothing happens.

"No," she repeats, voice breaking. "It's gone."

The world shifts sideways.

"What?" I ask, but I already know.

Her magic is gone. The poison didn't kill her, sure, but it destroyed her link to her magic. The Bright Waters healed her body, but they couldn't restore her powers. And if she can't access them, she can't re-erect the barrier. My stomach lurches as the truth settles on me.

"You're sure?" I ask desperately. "You've been in a coma for days, maybe your body just needs more time to wake up."

She looks at me, tears in her eyes.

"It's like reaching for water at the bottom of an empty well," she tells me sadly. "There is nothing to access."

Silence falls across the room for a long moment as we all try to think, try not to give into the fear that's hovering over all of us.

Akin is the first to speak.

"The barrier is still holding," he murmurs, walking to the window to look out.

"For now," Permiton answers, his eyes closed as he searches his Sight. "But it won't last forever. Our enemies will have it destroyed in a matter of days. How did I not see this coming?"

"There must be a precedent for this," Brook says, stepping back. "As long as the barrier is still up, we have a little time. I'll check the library for something we may have missed. We can fix this."

He turns to me for confirmation, and though he doesn't say it, I hear it anyway.

Maybe you're the one who has to do it.

River's already pacing.

"We should prepare for the worst. The army won't wait. They'll begin their attack as soon as they're given the order."

"How long do we have?" I ask.

Permiton's eyes close briefly.

"Hours," he says gravely. "Maybe less."

My breath catches.

"They're that close?"

"They're just waiting for the rest of Diereken's forces to arrive before they mount their full attack," he tells us.

So that's it, then. All of that traveling, all of that fighting against the hands of fate, and we've lost before we even had a chance to fight. Our enemies are closing in around us, and they will bring down the barrier. There's no way to stop the impending storm.

We are out of time.

THE MOMENTS BEFORE

River

After the revelation that Queen Kimalissa's magic is gone, everyone disperses to deal with the implications. Brook and Permiton have disappeared to the library to see if they can find any precedent for what's happening. Akin has disappeared to the barracks to be of service to the other soldiers in any way he can. Once again, I'm left without any real purpose.

So, I stand on the balcony of the palace, stone cold beneath my hands, and watch as the enemy armies spread across the distant hills. The blue and silver streamers of the Oceana flags catch the wind, their metallic edges reflecting the sun like blades. They aren't alone. Diereken's forces from Ambrosia march at their flank, cloaked in crimson.

The barrier hums weakly in the distance, stretched thin and ready to break at any moment. It's holding for now, but barely. One bad blow, and the whole thing could collapse. Maerilee doesn't think she's strong enough to fix it. She doesn't trust herself, and maybe she doesn't trust us. Or more likely, she still doesn't trust me. But she has to realize she's Altinna's last option.

Footsteps sound behind me and I turn to see Permiton walking toward me.

"They're closer than expected," he says as he joins me at the balcony's edge. "They've moved up the southern ridge. Your people are making excellent time."

"They're not *my* people," I mutter. "Not anymore."

He doesn't respond to that. He just looks out at the line of distant soldiers spreading across the valley. His expression is unreadable, but the tension in his jaw speaks volumes.

"I saw a vision of Eirliwyn with them," he says matter-of-factly. "He nearly killed the queen. He's probably come to finish the job."

"Have you told her?" I ask. "He's tricky, isn't he? He deals in shadow magic."

Permiton glances at me, a flicker of concern passing through his gaze.

"He does," Permiton confirms. "But the council is still reeling from his betrayal, and they don't trust me. Will you come with me to warn them?"

I simply nod, grateful to be of some use, and we turn from the balcony and head toward the war room. Inside is like a powder keg on the verge of explosion. Generals bark over one another, fingers jabbing at maps, shifting markers like they'll change reality if they yell loud enough. Half the table is arguing to reinforce the outer wall. The other half wants to retreat to the second ring of defense. All of them sound like they've given up and they're just strategizing their contingency plans.

At the head of the table, Maerilee sits still as stone, her expression unreadable. Otherwise, she seems composed and graceful, what a queen ought to be. But I know she's terrified. It's like I can feel her own fear inside of me. Everything will come down to her. As the future queen, the outcome of this war will affect whether or not she has a kingdom left to rule.

She catches my eye for the briefest moment, and I see a flicker of self-doubt. She can't show it to anyone but her Four. Anyone else would question her authority if she did. Gods, she's trying to be strong, but she isn't ready for this. None of us are.

I keep my eye on her as the men around her tear the kingdom into theoretical pieces, already dividing what little resources may remain if we lose.

Queen Kimalissa sits at Maerilee's right. She hasn't said much either, but her knuckles are white around the edge of the table. King Fratino is pacing near the map, rubbing a hand over his mouth.

I step closer to the table and raise my voice so I can be heard over the fray.

"Diereken's forces are close behind Oceana," I say, loud enough to cut through the chaos. "And Eirliwyn is with them. Permiton saw him in a vision."

The room goes eerily quiet as the men consider what this means. I look back over to Queen Kimalissa who is paler at the sound of her former advisor's name. He was closer to her than any of her advisors, yet he betrayed her and tried to kill her. His actions caused her to lose her magic. This war has become very personal for her.

Brook, surprisingly, is the first to speak, his voice quieter but firmer than usual. I didn't even realize he was here at first, but that's what I get for continuing to overlook my brother.

"We should use the terrain to funnel them into the kingdom," he says confidently, pointing to the map. "The ridge narrows on the western edge. We can use that to our advantage. It'll force them to break formation, and then we can strike more easily."

The generals consider this for a moment and whisper among themselves. Even I have to admit, it's a good plan. When did Brook become so good at military strategies?"

Permiton steps up beside him.

"They'll strike at night. That much is clear. Diereken and Eirliwyn both favor darkness. It hides their magic and weakens ours."

"Then we burn the paths," I offer. "Smoke them out, blind them instead."

Some of the generals nod. Others look unsure. And Maerilee still says nothing.

My hands tighten into fists at my sides, out of tension more than anything. Their forces greatly outnumber ours and we all know it. Even if Brook's plan works, they have a huge advantage in their sheer size.

The queen and king have sent out a signal for help from their allies, but so far no help has come. Many are still wary after the events of Maerilee's ball. All of this is because she's bound to four of us, and there's nothing we can do to change that. Even with all of our squabbles, I couldn't give her up if I tried.

I'm about to speak up when the doors to the chamber slam open and a scout stumbles in. He's bloodied, breathless, and one side of his uniform is torn open. He falls to his knees just inside the threshold, panting like he's run straight from the mouth of hell.

"Your Highness," his voice breaks. "They're moving faster than we thought. Diereken's beasts tore through the forest. Our scouts didn't have time to signal."

Everyone in the room freezes in panic and fear.

"They'll be at the barrier by nightfall," the scout manages before collapsing on the floor.

War is no longer coming. It's here.

AKIN

I WALK THROUGH THE CASTLE TO FIND MAERILEE, DISCONCERTED BY the quiet I find. It isn't a comforting sort of quiet at all. Everyone is off somewhere preparing for the impending war, and there's a deep tension and fear in this silence. I left the soldiers who were all pretending to be ready for what's to come, but we all know the truth. We have no chance at winning this war. We all know it deep down in our bones.

My boots echo through the corridor, slower now as I reach the royal wing. In another time, my heart would skip at the thought of seeing Maerilee, though before I would have to pretend that I didn't have feelings for her. Gods, we had so little time to enjoy being together. If we do lose this war, this might be our last chance.

I pause just outside her door. I don't even have to knock. The door opens soundlessly, and she's standing there in a simple gown, her hair falling over her shoulders like white silk. Her eyes meet mine, and for a moment, we just stare at each other silently. She holds out her hand, and I allow her to pull me inside. She closes the door behind me without a word.

The fire in the hearth casts a low glow across the room, but it's not warm enough to chase away the cold I've carried with me all day. There's an icy pit in my chest, reminding me that by morning, I might not be here. None of us may survive this, even though we can't say it out loud for fear that it will definitely come true if we do.

She crosses to the edge of the bed and sits, folding her hands in her lap. She doesn't look at me at first, just stares at the floor, her own private war waging behind her eyes.

"I didn't think we'd lose before we even had a chance to fight," she says after a long silence. "We went through so much to save my mother, and now it doesn't even matter."

I move toward her slowly.

"Of course it matters," I say carefully. "Queen Kimalissa is alive because of you, because of your tenacity. And that will get you through whatever comes next."

When I sit beside her, she leans into me automatically. I lift my arm around her shoulders, anchoring her against me, and for a few minutes, we just breathe. The world could come to an end outside of this room, and we probably wouldn't notice. At least, at first. There is only Maerilee and I and the love between us.

She tilts her head to look at me.

"Are you afraid?" she asks in a whisper.

I hesitate because I don't want my own fear to scare her more. I'd like to tell her I'm confident and that everything will be okay. But even if I did lie to her, she'd know immediately. So, I don't try to hide my true feelings from her.

"Yes," I say softly. "I'm afraid."

Her lips part slightly, but she doesn't interrupt.

"I'm afraid I won't be able to protect you." I finally express the worst fear that's been weighing me down. "More than losing the war, even of dying, I'm afraid of losing you, Maerilee."

She closes her eyes against my words and takes a steady breath.

"Thank you for being honest with me," she finally says in a steadier voice. "I'm not afraid of death, Akin, but I'm terrified of having to live without you. Without any of you."

Her amendment does nothing to stop the swelling of love in my chest. She is my entire world, and I will do anything I can to keep her safe. I bring her hand to my lips, kissing her knuckles one by one. The skin is soft there, delicate.

"I don't want to waste our precious time pretending I'm not terrified," she says, her voice barely above a whisper. "And I don't want to die without telling you how much I love you."

My throat tightens. She looks at me then, really looks, and everything in me stills.

"Maerilee," I protest, but it does nothing to stop her.

"You have always meant the world to me, Akin," she continues, her voice starting to break with emotion. "So if we don't make it out of this alive–"

"Don't," I murmur, leaning closer and cutting her off with a kiss. "Don't even think it. Don't give me a last goodbye before we've even fought."

She exhales shakily, pressing her forehead to mine.

"Then just stay with me until we have to go down to the battlefield."

"I will," I say. "Until the very last second."

I kiss her again, though I try deliberately to keep my own desperation out of the kiss. After what I've just said, I don't want my body to betray me by making this feel like a goodbye. We take the time that we don't have, memorizing each other one more time. I dare not think one last time, but it's there in the back of my mind.

When she reaches for the clasp of my armor, I let her. Piece by piece, I shed it for her. She removes my chest plate, my gloves, and my chainmail. I don't rush her and she doesn't rush me. If this really will be our last time together, we will savor every single second we still have.

She peels away the last layer of cloth between us, her fingers slow and trembling. I reach for the tie of her gown and slip it loose, letting the fabric fall from her shoulders.

She is as beautiful as ever, maybe even more so in the glow of my pre-war anxieties. Her flesh prickles as I slowly kiss every inch that I can reach. Her fingers instinctively grasp at the nape of my neck as she relaxes back onto the bed, allowing me to have this, to taste her how I need to.

"If this isn't goodbye, let this be a promise," she says in a breathy gasp. "When this is all over, we'll never be parted."

"Never," I whisper against the dip in her hips as I kiss lower. "I am yours, forever, Maerilee."

"And I'm yours," she says, crooking a finger under my chin and forcing me to look up at her. "But time isn't on our side, so you'd better get back up here."

I match her wicked grin, crawling slowly back up her body, rubbing myself against her so I can feel every last inch of her skin. When I reach her mouth, I press my lips against hers with all of the love and passion I can possibly infuse in a single kiss. I try to convey with my actions, rather than my words, how much she means to me.

Her touch is just as fierce, and our bodies meld together into one until it's impossible for me to tell where she ends and I begin. I feel her shudder as I enter her, and every nerve in my body relaxes the moment I'm inside of her, where I feel the most at peace.

We move together in a frantic rhythm, equally trying to make the moment last forever and find our bliss before we're inevitably interrupted. As she said, time is not on our side, and I can't walk into battle without feeling her come undone around me at least one more time.

I shift us, pulling her on top of me in the way I know she likes. She rides me hard and fast, her body nearly vibrating with pleasure. My hands ground her hips, as she moves on top of me, gasping with every movement. I'm careening on the edge of pleasure as I feel her tighten around me, her body tensing with pleasure.

"I love you, Akin," she whispers over and over as she rides her high, collapsing on top of me in exhaustion.

I hold her against my chest for a long while, stroking her long white hair until the sun starts to get lower. War is upon us, but I will walk into battle cherishing every second of our time together.

THE FIRST WAVE

Akin

THE SUN SETS BEHIND THE TREES, TURNING THE SKY THE COLOR OF blood. I shudder to think what this battlefield will look like when the sun reemerges. How many of us will still be standing?

I'm at the front line, shoulder to shoulder with the generals, watching the tree line just beyond the barrier. The wind rustles the leaves like a sinister whisper, the promise of death. My fingers tighten around the hilt of my sword, ready to strike any target at a moment's notice. As much as we've trained for years, this is the first time many of us will ever face direct conflict with another kingdom. The burden of that knowledge settles on all of us as we wait with anticipation for the coming armies.

Behind us is the barrier. We are the last defense to keep the Oceanans and Ambrosians from destroying it. If it falls now, all will be lost. We've got all of our strongest men ready to sacrifice their lives to keep the opposing soldiers back. And still, I don't know if it will be enough.

River stands to my right, unusually still for a man who rarely stops moving. He's been more serious than I've ever seen him, and I was honestly surprised he volunteered to be at the front. Whether it was stubborn pride or a need to prove himself, I may never know. But he turns to me and nods, his eyes dark and dangerous.

His jaw ticks. His hands clench and release. He's trying to rein in whatever anger is brewing beneath the surface. I can see the way his eyes search the horizon, like if he stares hard enough, he'll catch the enemy before they appear. These are his people, or at least they once were. I can't imagine how hard it must be for him to fight against them.

Brook is further back, near the final support line, his hands held high in a defensive pose. Water swirls at his fingertips, tight and controlled. He's watching too, but he looks more thoughtful than tense. Focused. These two former princes are willing to sacrifice themselves for the good of a kingdom that doesn't recognize them. All because of the woman we all love. It's hard not to feel a kinship with them, despite our previous spats.

Permiton stands like a statue near the edge of the line, one hand raised to his temple, his eyes clouded with his Sight. His expression is unfocused as he searches the future for any sort of answer. I know he wants to protect us the best way he can, and that means using his gift to give us an advantage. He might not be our strongest soldier in a fight, but his gift is an asset we desperately need.

The rest of the soldiers shift around me uneasily. The younger men are so afraid, I can see their hands shaking as they grip their swords. The elder fae are more steady, but no less tense. No one knows what to expect, exactly. No one speaks. No one dares break the silence.

I roll my shoulders once, stretching out the tension that's building there. I think of Maerilee's face as pleasure took over her earlier. For just a moment, she was as calm and relaxed as anyone could possibly be. I look back toward the barrier. She stands just behind it, protected as much as she can be. I fight for her. We all do.

But we are not prepared for what will happen tonight. None of us have ever been in such a dangerous position. Commander Heela's cruelty is still burned into my memory. At the thought, my wrists start to burn with the phantom feeling of the special ropes he'd used to bind me. If it weren't for Permiton's quick thinking and Caelan's rebels, he would have killed all of us. It's our turn to return his cruelty pound for pound.

Behind the barrier, beyond the stronghold, I can almost feel Maerilee's presence. She's there, watching with her chin lifted and her shoulders straight. Despite what we shared with each other, neither one of us can show an ounce of weakness now. Our fear is irrelevant on the battlefield.

I close my eyes and imagine her next to me, her hand in mine. I know that's exactly where she would be if her position allowed for it.

"I love you," I whisper to her, though I know she can't hear. Part of me hopes she can still sense it from where she is. I swallow hard, then open my eyes again.

The trees are still. The sun has nearly vanished now, just a sliver of gold clinging to the edge of the world. And then the horn sounds, deep and low. It rolls across the battlefield like thunder.

"Form up!" one of the generals bellows. "Shields forward!"

The front line tightens. Steel glints in the last light. My own sword slides from its sheath with a hiss that cuts through the growing noise.

Magic crackles to my left. River is already lit with it, his water swirling like smoke around his arms, his jaw clenched. We watch the tree line with all of our concentration, ready to strike the moment the first soldier steps a foot onto the field.

Then the branches part and they flood out of the tree line like a crashing wave. Oceanan warriors pour from the forest in tight, fast-moving ranks. Their armor is lacquered black, their water magic already swirling around. Water whips around them like serpents, lashing the air, the earth, anything in their path.

I shout, lift my sword, and then the front line is moving as one unit as we crash forward to meet them. The sound of impact is deafening, steel against steel, magic against flesh. There are horrible screams, roars of pain, the thunder of boots, the crack of shields, the burst of water magic erupting like cannon fire through the lines. It's impossible to know which side is taking more heat as we collide, becoming a tangle of opposing forces.

I duck a blade, sweep low, and drive my sword up into the gap beneath an enemy's ribs. The man gurgles and drops. Another takes his place. I spin, block, drive forward again. Blood splashes across my face and I don't even know if it's mine. I just keep swinging, trading blow for blow with whichever Oceanan soldier happens to get in my way.

Our line is holding for now, every soldier fighting as hard as they can to keep the Oceanan army at bay. The line doesn't break, but we're only just at the beginning and it's already chaos. I truly don't know how much more we can take.

A spell explodes close to my left, forcing me to duck. I see the shockwave ripple and knock one of our archers clean off the barricade. River shouts something I can't make out. Brook's magic surges, a wall of ice forming in a blink as he deflects a strike that would have gutted three of our soldiers. Permiton remains eerily still, away from the fighting, his eyes glowing faintly, his lips moving soundlessly. I don't know what he sees. I just hope it helps.

I keep fighting. My arm is already sore. My legs burn. I've barely drawn breath. But I don't stop. I can't stop. Another Oceanan charges. I parry high, then kick his leg out from under him, slamming the hilt of my blade into his jaw. He goes down. Another takes his place. They just keep coming. There's no end to them in sight, and the tide hasn't even peaked yet.

I grit my teeth and adjust my stance. My heart is pounding, but my mind is clear. I lift my blade again and brace for the next charge. I move like a force of nature. I don't think. I don't pause. I let my training guide me, the rhythm of battle familiar in my muscles, even as exhaustion presses in with every breath. My sword becomes an extension of my will. When I swing, they fall. When I move, my unit follows. We push, we strike, we hold.

I shout to one of the captains to hold the flank. He's bleeding from the shoulder but nods and disappears into the smoke. My chest heaves, sweat and blood soaking through my shirt beneath the armor. I can't stop now. If I stop, I die.

A flash of movement to my left, and I duck just in time as a blade whistles over my head. I pivot and drive my sword up through the ribs of a soldier barely older than a boy. His eyes widen. He slumps forward. I let him fall.

I turn just in time to block another strike. My sword clashes with a curved Oceanan blade, and the force of it vibrates all the way up my arm. I grunt and push forward, locking the man's sword beneath mine, then wrench it free and drive my boot into his stomach. He falls. Another rushes in behind him.

I can't tell if we're winning, but I don't think we are. My body moves through the chaos, reacting to danger before my mind can even register it. There's too much happening at once. Fire explodes behind me, throwing half a dozen soldiers to the ground. A scream cuts through the smoke, and I don't know if it's one of ours or theirs.

The air is thick with ash and fear. I manage to catch sight of Maerilee through the chaos of it all. She's just beyond the barrier, standing tall on the overlook with her white hair shining like moonlight through the smoke. She's watching, her eyes locked on the battlefield, scanning every movement. When she sees me, our eyes lock and for a moment, everything stops. Everything narrows.

My heart stumbles in my chest, but I keep moving, cutting through another Oceanan, stepping over a fallen Altinnian, trying to hold the line that is beginning to fray at the edges. Still, I can't look away. Not from her.

She doesn't blink. She doesn't flinch. She just watches.

I want to tell her to run. To stay hidden. But I know she won't do that. She would never abandon her people in the time of need. She's the one who keeps me going, who's keeping me fighting in the midst of this hell. For her and only her, I can't stop, can't even take a breath. I want to reach for her, but I don't get the chance.

An Oceanan lunges toward me from the side, blade raised, water magic coiling around his arms like whips. I twist, block the first strike, but another comes from behind. I'm surrounded. My boots slip in the mud. My sword catches one blow, deflects another. I grab one of them by the wrist and slam his head into my knee. He crumples, but now I'm off balance.

Another blade glances off my shoulder, cutting deep through leather and skin. I snarl and swing hard, taking him down with a wild arc. But there's no time to recover.

Fire comes quickly from our enemies. Flames erupt in a line across the field, disorienting and blinding. I stumble back coughing as my vision starts to swim. Magic slams into the ground near my feet, throwing earth and bodies into the air. I duck, roll, come up swinging, and barely avoid a spear meant for my chest.

Everything is chaos. I can no longer see where River is. Brook is somewhere to the left, casting spell after spell, his energy almost drained. I hope to the gods that Permiton saw this coming. He has completely disappeared from my vision, swallowed into the sea of bodies and the haze of smoke.

The Altinnian soldiers hold their positions, but their formation is splintering under the force of so many attacks. We've fought them as hard as we can, but it still may not be enough. There are so many more of them still to come, a mass of bodies that just doesn't stop coming. There is no end in sight.

I turn to find Maerilee again, still behind the barrier. Her hand is on the railing of the balcony where she's watching, and her mouth opens as if it's forming my name. Perhaps my name.

Then everything rushes toward us at once. Water crashes over the front line like a tidal wave summoned by a dozen Oceanan mages. Fire follows it, slicing through the fog in bright, lethal ribbons. Magic collides with steel. Earth cracks beneath my feet. Light and shadow swirl so fast it's impossible to tell who's winning.

I try to find her again… but I can't.

THE SPOILS OF BATTLE

Brook

The wind tastes like ash, carrying the smoke from the Ambrosian's attack. They're assembled behind the Oceanan soldiers, shooting their magic at us with wild abandon. I stand at the back of the Altinnian line, feet planted wide, arms raised, water already swirling at my fingertips. I never received the same training as River, was never taught to be as graceful or powerful as the Oceanan soldiers, but my magic listens to me, and that's all I can ask of it for now.

I pull from the well inside me, deeper than I've ever gone before, and send a blast of water arcing through the air. It catches two Oceanan soldiers before they reach the front line. One stumbles. The other skids across the mud, his blade slipping from frozen fingers.

Another enemy charges forward. I draw the water back, wrap it around his ankles, and snap it upward into a spear of ice. He doesn't rise again. I attack man after man, trying to protect as many Altinnian soldiers as I can from the onslaught of Oceanan warriors. But it's chaos now, and the smoke makes it harder and harder for me to see, to determine who's on our side and who is against us.

Every breath burns in my chest. My arms ache from keeping them lifted, but the magic keeps coming. It surges, clumsy but relentless, responding more to instinct than control. I use what I can and shape it however I know how.

Not for the first time, I resent my parents for refusing to let me train. They thought I was worthless, a spare to the very healthy and strong heir. They saw my strengths as being neither seen nor heard, so I spent my time in the royal libraries, learning everything I could. But book knowledge does nothing on the battlefield.

Fire crashes to my left. Someone screams. I don't turn. I can't afford to turn my gaze anywhere but toward my enemies. I send another wave of water toward the advancing Oceanans. It slams into their line, disrupting their momentum. Just a moment's pause, just enough for the front to regroup.

A man falls beside me, chest pierced with a broken spear. Bile rises up in my throat, but I have to swallow it down. My pulse slams behind my eyes. This is not the moment for weakness. I fight every instinct in my body that wants me to turn around and run for safety. There are just too many of them.

River fights near the front, his magic controlled, brutal. Every motion is deliberate, clean. He's a beast on the battlefield, using his military training against the very men who taught him how to hone his magic.

I draw more water from the air, the ground, my own blood if I have to. I summon a wall, jagged and cold, to slow the next rush. It shatters on impact, splinters flying. Two Altinnian soldiers fall behind me, another shouts for reinforcement. I stagger forward, muscles trembling.

The barrier behind us flickers again. The golden shimmer pulses weakly, then steadies. Maerilee is behind it, ready to erect a smaller barrier if necessary, but it will be nothing like this one. She can't protect the entire kingdom with her magic yet.

If this barrier breaks, the kingdom is lost.

A shout rises near the center of the field. The Oceanan army is reorganizing, forming into a second wave that's stronger and faster. Permiton's forces are catching up to the front line, ready to sub in as soon as they're needed. If they reach our front line, it's over.

I lift both hands and call on everything inside me. The wave I send this time is larger and thicker than anything I've ever conjured before. It's a tidal wave, ready to take out anyone in its path. I freeze it midair and slam it into the line of Oceanan soldiers rushing toward the eastern flank. It hits hard. Men fall. Ice explodes into mist. For one brief moment, they retreat, but it isn't enough.

A third wave follows, and the Altinnian line starts to break apart. I turn, trying to hold the center with another blast of ice, but I am too slow.

I see River take a hit to the shoulder. He snarls and returns fire, but even he is being pushed back now. The ground beneath our feet has turned to muck, blood and water churning beneath our boots.

I lift my arm again to cast anything I possibly can, but the magic is waning. My own body is turning against me, exhaustion overtaking me. But before I even have a chance, I feel a blade go through my chest.

I do not see the man who does it, only the glint of steel out of the corner of my eye, but the pain is instant. I feel like I'm being torn in half as I feel the blade pulled from my chest. I stagger backward, breath vanishing from my lungs, vision narrowing to a tight, swimming blur. My knees buckle. The water at my fingertips vanishes.

I hear someone scream my name. And then there's nothing.

❀

River

. . .

I HEAR MAERILEE'S BLOOD CURDLING SCREAM PIERCE THE BATTLEFIELD before I see what it is that has her so afraid. I whip around just as my name tears from her throat, but she's not looking at me.

She's looking at Brook.

"River, help him!" she cries louder, forcing me into action.

My stomach twists and my blood turns to ice as I see my brother at the back of the line, crumpled to the ground and bleeding out.

"Brook," I whisper, unable to find the breath to scream.

Something shatters inside me and I'm running for my life, faster than I thought capable, to get to my brother.

The battlefield moves around me in jagged blurs. Soldiers on every side are screaming in pain, bodies are strewn across the mud, but I hardly see any of it. The only thing I see is my little brother lying motionless in the dirt, the front of his tunic already stained dark.

An Oceanan soldier stands over him, his blade raised for a second strike. I don't even stop to think. I call the water to me from every fiber of the land. It wraps around my arm in a perfect arc and shoots forward like a whip. It slams into the soldier's chest with enough force to lift him off his feet. He falls and doesn't get up. I hope he's dead.

I reach Brook in the next breath, fall to my knees, and gather him into my arms.

His head lolls against my shoulder, his face pale beneath streaks of ash and blood. His eyes are half-open, unfocused, his mouth parted like he's trying to speak but can't remember how.

My fingers come away slick with far too much blood.

"No," I whisper, cupping the back of his head. "No, no, no! Brook, look at me. Hey. Look at me."

He doesn't.

"Brook," I scream, his name in my mouth. "You stubborn, soft-hearted bastard, don't you dare die. Don't you dare!"

His breathing is shallow. In and out. Faint. Unsteady.

The battlefield screams around us, but it all fades. None of it matters now. Not the war. Not the barrier. Not even Maerilee. The only thing that matters is the weight of my brother going slack in my arms.

I grip him tighter, slide one arm beneath his knees, the other behind his back. My legs are already burning, my shoulder bleeding, but I lift him anyway. I don't care what it costs me. He is still breathing. I can still save him.

I'm running again, all thoughts of the battle pushed from my mind. I don't look back toward the soldiers fighting. I'm moving toward the barrier, toward safety.

The barrier's shimmer glows faintly ahead, its magic flickering like a dying lantern. I race toward it. Brook's body is heavy against mine, his head pressed to my chest, his blood soaking into my uniform, into my skin. I already know it's too much blood, that his life is hanging in the balance.

I won't let him die. I won't fail him. Not this time.

Maerilee meets me the second I cross the barrier. Her hands reach for Brook, but she doesn't try to take him. Her face is white, eyes wide, wild with fear.

"Do something," she screams. "River, you have to do something!"

Her voice cracks, a desperate, feral sound ripping from her chest. My heart breaks, not just for her pain but for mine. Despite everything, I love Brook as much as she does. He is the only family I have left in this world. He saved my life.

And that's when I remember the vial of Bright Waters I have hidden in my tunic. The weight of despair lifts off of me for just the briefest moment.

I set Brook down gently on the ground, cradle his head in my lap, and dig into the pouch at my belt. My fingers close around the glass before I fully register what I'm doing. I pull it free.

The liquid inside glows softly, a blue so pure it almost hurts to look at it. Without thinking, I bite down on the cork, pulling it off with my teeth.

"I saved it for him," I whisper to Maerilee, my voice thick. "He used his vial to save me, and I promised him I would save mine for him."

I tip the vial to Brook's lips.

"Come on," I murmur. "Just a little. Please."

The first drop hits his tongue, but nothing happens. Another drop falls on his lips, and I see his throat move. He swallows just once. I slowly pour the rest of the vial into his mouth, desperate for it to bring him back from the brink of death.

For a heartbeat, there's nothing. He doesn't move or breathe, and I worry I was too late. If Brook dies, I might as well march back down to that battlefield and take a sword to my chest. I don't want to live in this world without him. Maerilee begins to sob, but I go numb, unable to feel or do anything for the moment.

Then Brook's chest rises faintly. He takes in a shallow breath, then gasps for air like he's been under water. He coughs once and blinks. His fingers twitch in mine.

Maerilee drops to her knees on his other side, clutching his hand, tears spilling down her cheeks. She says his name over and over again like it's the only thing holding him to this world. His eyes flutter open, just for a moment, and they find her. Then his head lazily moves to the side and he looks at me. He takes another deep breath.

Relief crashes into me like a wave. I bow my head, my forehead touching his, my hand still on his chest, feeling the life beneath my palm.

"I've got you," I whisper. "You're okay. You're okay. You're okay."

Maerilee sobs quietly, pressing her lips to his temple. I don't stop her. I don't say anything at all.

After a few moments, her gaze lifts to mine.

"You have to take him to the castle," she says, voice hoarse. "He needs care. He needs to be somewhere safe."

I nod without argument. I remember how weak I felt after the Bright Waters saved me. Brook needs to rest, and the castle is the last possible refuge we have.

I slide my arms under him again, gentler now, more cautious. He groans softly, and it's the most beautiful sound I've ever heard.

"I've got you," I say again, more to myself than him.

I rise slowly, carefully. My muscles are screaming at me, my body more sore than it's ever been, but I have to get Brook to safety. Maer-ilee puts a hand on my forearm, forcing me to look at her. Her eyes meet mine. And in them, I see the war still raging behind her, the burden on her shoulders, the cracks forming in her resolve.

"Thank you, River," she barely manages.

I nod to her once, then make my way back to the castle, saying a silent prayer the whole way.

LOST

Akin

I have never felt fear like this in my life. The Oceanans are everywhere, relentless, swarming us on all sides. I can barely see two feet in front of me through the wall of bodies and smoke and flaring magic.

There's no formation to our soldiers now, no real lines left. We are hardly an army at all now, just soldiers fighting for their lives, one man against five or more Oceanans at one time. The only thing keeping this army from swallowing us whole is the barrier still shimmering weakly at our backs. We will retreat if we must, but there's the very real possibility that the barrier will not hold up against our enemies. We have to fight them back as long as we possibly can... which, I fear, isn't much longer.

I fight. That is all I know how to do. I swing and block and press forward, my sword a blur in my hands, my muscles screaming with every movement. My boots slide in the blood-slicked mud. My shoulder throbs from a blade I didn't deflect fast enough. My lungs burn with smoke.

Still, I do not stop.

Men become blurs to me, just limbs and weapons I have to deflect. As long as they're in the Oceanan colors, I do not think. I only strike.

I'm surrounded at all sides, with no relief in sight. For all I know, I'm the last man standing. At least that's how it feels in the midst of all of these Oceanans.

Somewhere behind me, I hear River yelling. Then I do not hear him at all. I turn, just for a second, but he is gone, lost to the blur of motion and magic and screaming. He could be dead, for all I know. There's no way for me to know.

I keep going alone. An enemy soldier lunges toward one of ours. I intercept, driving my blade through his stomach. He crumples, already dead before he hits the ground. We are being pushed back slowly and relentlessly, a tide dragging us toward the barrier inch by inch.

I don't care about myself. I only care that the enemy does not reach Maerilee. I keep pushing forward for her. Blindly, I press on, killing more men than I can possibly count. But then, for one horrible instant, I am too slow.

I do not see the blade before it buries itself deep into my side. The pain is instant, sharp and hot, blooming through my ribs like fire. My body jerks with the force of it. My breath catches.

But I refuse to fall.

I grit my teeth and swing my sword one more time, slashing through the throat of the warrior who stabbed me. He drops beside me, his blood joining mine in the mud. I press my hand to my side, but it does nothing. My tunic is already soaked through.

My vision waivers and the world begins to tilt. I plant my feet and press forward.

Another enemy crashes into me. I push him back, slam my elbow into his face, and turn and slash at another. Every motion feels heavier than the one before. My body is beginning to fail me, but I keep moving.

Then another blade finds me, and this one goes deeper. I feel it all the way to the bone. My knees buckle. The ground rushes up toward me. My fingers loosen. My sword slips from my grasp.

I land hard, the impact jarring through my spine. My hand

searches for my weapon, but I can't find it. My arm won't move the way I tell it to.

Everything blurs. Around me, the battle rages on. Screams echo. Magic explodes. Steel sings against steel. But it all feels distant. Drowned out. Like the battlefield is fading away from me, even though I am still in the center of it.

Then a solitary sound reaches my ears. Maerilee is screaming my name, her voice raw and terrified, and I know it's much worse than I think.

I try to lift my head, but it is too heavy. I try to speak, to call back to her, but nothing comes out. I spit out blood instead of words.

My eyes find her beyond the barrier, and I try to find a way to convey to her to stay where she is. If these are my last moments, I have to know she's safe. I will not watch her die.

She steps out from behind the safety of the golden shimmer and starts to run.

No.

I want to scream at her to go back. To stay behind the barrier. But I cannot make a sound.

Then I see Permiton running toward her. He grabs her, and holds her back with as much strength as he can manage. She fights him, but he is stronger. She claws at his arm, shouting for him to let go as she tries desperately to reach me.

He doesn't. It's like his last gift to me. I can't see his face as he drags Maerilee away, but I thank him silently for getting her away from the danger. He pulls her back to safety. Back behind the magic that still holds.

I lie in the dirt, broken and bleeding, and I watch the woman I love scream for me with her whole soul. Our eyes meet one last time. She is frozen in place now, tears streaking her face, her mouth forming my name again and again.

And I reach for her. My arm lifts an inch. That is all I can manage. It trembles in the air, hand outstretched. A dozen images flash in my mind, all of them of her. I remember the first time we met, when I was appointed to her personal guard. I remember the years of pretending my interest in her was purely professional. I remember the first time we kissed, when we made love and we knew that we were destined for one another.

I was born to love her. I was trained to protect her. Now I will die for her, and it will be the greatest honor.

Shadows begin to creep around me, cold and thick, wrapping around me like a second skin.

They rise from the ground, curl around my limbs, and drag me down. I cannot fight them. I have nothing left. In my delirium, I wonder if they're real, or if this is what everyone envisions when they die. Death comes for all of us in the end, after all.

The last thing I see before the shadows swallow me whole is Maerilee's face, her silver eyes wide with helpless horror.

Maerilee

I STOP BREATHING. AKIN FALLS, AND THE WORLD STOPS MOVING. Everything else on the battlefield, the fire, the screaming, the wave of enemy soldiers closing in… it all blurs into silence. My eyes lock on Akin, just as his body hits the ground.

No.

I don't think. My body moves before my mind catches up, a scream ripping out of me, loud and wild and raw. I run to the edge of the barrier. To him.

I can still see him. He is still there, lying helplessly on the ground. If I can get to him, if I can just reach him, this won't be the end. He and Permiton still have their Bright Waters. We can still save him the way River saved Brook. He's going to be okay.

I don't make it far. Arms wrap around me from behind, hard and unyielding. I look behind me to see Permiton holding me in a vice grip. He drags me back with a strength I didn't know he had, hauling me away back to the barrier like I am no heavier than a child. I thrash in his grip, clawing at him, screaming for him to let go.

"You don't understand," I sob, fighting against him with everything I have. "He is still alive. He can still be saved."

"Maerilee," Permiton grits through his teeth. "You have to get back behind the barrier. If they see you, they will kill you."

"I don't care," I cry. "He is out there. He is bleeding. You still have your Bright Waters. You can save him like River saved Brook. Please. Permiton. Please."

He stops pulling. I spin on him, desperate and trembling.

"It's not too late," I whisper. "Please, Permiton, save him!"

Permiton's face twists with pain, and he slowly nods.

"I'll go to him, but you have to promise me you'll stay behind the barrier."

"I swear," I rasp, my voice barely holding together. "Please. Go."

He lets go of me and turns. I turn too, and the world crumbles. Akin's body is swallowed up into shadows.

One second he is there, lying in the mud, arm outstretched toward me. The next, he's just gone, disappeared from the battlefield.

I don't understand what I am seeing. I cannot move, cannot breathe.

"No," I whisper. Then I scream it. "No!"

I stumble forward, hand pressed to the barrier, staring at the empty space where he was.

"No. No. No. No."

Permiton stumbles back to my side, his face pale and horrified. He saw it happen too. There is nothing he can say or do. Akin is gone. He isn't just dead. He has vanished.

I sink to my knees, my hands clenched in the dirt, the breath gone from my lungs.

He is gone.

Gone.

My mouth opens, and a scream tears loose from somewhere deep inside me. It shakes the entire earth, even causing the barrier to tremble. It is not of this world, not a sound that even makes sense coming from my body. It's not just in my lungs, but in the air, in the ground, coming from the sky.

It sounds like everything I have ever loved being ripped away.

I scream again and again and there are no more words, no more breath. There's only magic.

It builds without warning or thought. I don't call or summon it, it just comes from deep down inside of me, from some ancient place.

It pours out of me like lightning through my veins. The ground vibrates beneath me. My hair lifts in the air, crackling with power. The air shimmers with golden light.

Then the magic erupts. It surges from my chest in a wave, blinding and hot and full of grief. It races across the battlefield in a brilliant arc, a dome of force that slams into the Oceanan army like a physical blow.

Every last one of them falls, warriors being knocked off their feet. Mages are thrown backward through the smoke. The line buckles and breaks as all of the soldiers from Oceana and Ambrosia crumble at once.

The battlefield goes silent. I hear one of the generals call out to the soldiers, but it sounds a million miles away.

"Fall back! Fall back behind the barrier!"

No one hesitates or questions him. The soldiers move fast, retreating behind the faltering barrier, their eyes wide with fear and awe. They carry the wounded. They drag the dying. They do not speak.

Our enemies cannot follow. They are still knocked unconscious from the wave of magic that surged through me without my permission. I kneel in the dirt, unable to move, unable to feel anything but the hollow ache of Akin's death.

I do not know how to keep living without him.

AN IMPOSSIBLE ASK

MAERILEE

OCEANAN SOLDIERS ARE SPRAWLED IN UNNATURAL SHAPES ACROSS churned earth and stone, their limbs slack, faces limp with unconsciousness. None of them are dead. I can feel that, somewhere in the strange bond between my magic and the land. But they are incapacitated, stunned by the burst of power that tore out of me moments ago like it had been waiting all along to be freed. No one speaks. No one moves. It feels like the world is holding its breath.

But all I can think is that Akin is gone.

I stare at the space where he fell, where he reached for me, but it is empty. He was there. I know he was. I saw him. Permiton saw him. Permiton was going to go back for him so we could revive him. Yet now he is gone, and something inside me feels like it has been ripped away at the roots.

Somehow, I end up in the courtyard of the palace. I don't remember moving here, and I have no recollection of leaving my place behind the barrier. My gown is torn, my hands are scraped raw from the ground, and my breath is so jagged it comes in shudders instead of rhythm. I can feel the rough stone beneath my knees, the cold seep of it against my skin, but I cannot find the strength to lift my head.

Everything around me has gone dim and distant. Shadows are moving around me, soldiers, perhaps, but I am not aware of them. They may have faces, but to me they are all darkness. Nothing matters anymore. Akin is gone. There is no light left in this world.

River's voice pierces through the ringing in my ears, but it barely makes a dent. I hear him shout, demanding to know what happened, the words sharp and frightened in a way that surprises me. Permiton answers him, though I can't make out the details. The words come muffled, as though they are underwater, as though I am underwater, too deep and too tired to swim to the surface.

And then Mother is there. I know her scent before her hands touch me. Lavender, and old parchment, and a trace of the oils she rubs into her temples when her headaches become unbearable. She kneels beside me, her hands warm on my face, her voice low and urgent.

"Maerilee," she says, and though her tone is gentle, there is steel beneath it.

I look up at her, barely recognizing the pain in her eyes because I am so submerged in my own. But her arms come around me, and I let myself fall into them like I did when I was small and scraped my knee on the castle stairs. I break then, all the way. My breath catches and releases in sobs I can no longer hold back, and I bury my face in her shoulder like the child I once was, because she is the only anchor I have left in this moment.

"He was right there," I whisper, again and again. "Where has he gone?"

She says nothing for a long moment, only holding me tighter, her own breath unsteady. When she speaks, her voice is as raw as mine.

"I know, my heart. I know."

I do not know how long we stay like that. The air smells like smoke and ash, and a weak light is starting to pierce through the clouds. Daylight is coming, but how can there be daylight when my world has ended? Behind us, I hear the murmurs of soldiers regrouping, the rustle of armor, the scrape of blades being sheathed. It is only when one of the generals approaches that I begin to stir.

"Your Majesty," the general says, not to me, but to my mother. His voice is clipped with urgency. "The Oceanans are waking. Not all, but enough. And the barrier is unstable at best. Time is of the essence, ma'am. We have to act fast to protect our people."

My mother breathes in slowly, and I feel the motion of it under my cheek. Then she pulls back enough to look me in the eyes. She doesn't raise her voice. She doesn't give commands. She only holds my face in her hands and speaks to me as her daughter.

"Maerilee, I know this is the last thing you want to hear. But I need you."

I blink at her, my vision swimming.

"I don't know what I can do," I breathe helplessly. "I have nothing left."

"You do," she assures me, with more certainty than I can understand. "You have already done the impossible. I do not know what kind of power you released out there, but it saved us. It bought us time. And now you must use what is left of that power to protect the people. The barrier that's still holding won't last. You need to create a smaller one, just around the castle. Give them somewhere to shelter."

I shake my head slowly.

"I can't do it, Mother. Not without him."

"Yes," she says, her voice firmer now. "Even without him. Especially because he's gone. Maerilee, Akin gave his life to protect this kingdom. You have to honor his sacrifice now."

I don't respond right away. I stare at her, at the smudges under her eyes, the soft new lines of age that have deepened without me noticing. I see her strength, and I remember who I am supposed to become. I'm not just her daughter. I am the future queen of Altinna. I have to lead my people, to protect my people, even if I can't find the will to keep living for myself.

Before I can gather myself, River kneels beside me. He doesn't speak at first. He only rests a hand on my shoulder, his fingers grounding and steady. There is something in his face that has shifted since last night. Even he looks older somehow. I don't know what changed in him.

"I'll help," he says quietly. "Whatever you need."

Permiton steps forward then, his expression drawn and pale. He looks exhausted, his usually sharp eyes dull around the edges, like he too has seen too much. But he nods once, solemn and steady.

"You're not alone, Maerilee."

And I believe him.

With trembling limbs, I rise. My body protests, but I ignore it. I walk with them toward the far edge of the courtyard, where the walls curve outward into the open space that overlooks the castle grounds. I look out over the city, the rooftops shimmering in the dying light, the people beginning to gather, their voices hushed and fearful. The old barrier still flickers at the far edge of the horizon, but it is thinner now, barely holding. Beyond that, I can still feel the presence of the Oceanans as they begin to regroup.

I reach inside myself, searching for the source of my power. It feels different now. Still raw, still wild, but deeper, as though something has broken open and made room for more. I do not know how to use it. I only know it is there.

I close my eyes. River takes one of my hands. Permiton takes the other and together, we channel it. The magic builds slowly, gathering in my chest, blooming outward like a flower unfolding. It stretches through my arms, across my skin, into the space around us. I feel the castle's heartbeat, the pulse of the land under our feet. I call to it, ask it to protect what remains.

The barrier rises.

Not as large as the one around the kingdom. This one is tighter and closer knit, wrapped only around the castle and the immediate grounds. It shimmers gold and silver, faintly pulsing with my heartbeat. It holds strong, its power humming with more force than its predecessor. It isn't much, but the castle is large enough to protect the citizens once the barrier falls. It is enough.

I fall to my knees once again, but this time, I am caught. River pulls me gently against him. Permiton murmurs something I cannot quite hear. The barrier stands. The people are protected.

PERMITON

Every door in the castle is manned, every window is watched. The corridors echo with shouts and whispered instructions as scouts usher all of Altinna's civilians into the castle. It all happened so quickly. If this army is anything, it is efficient. The moment Maerilee put up the boundary around the castle, the exhausted men went house to house throughout the kingdom, gathering every citizen and instructing them to get to the castle as soon as possible. There was no time to wait, or think, or question.

I watch them pass through the gates, families clinging to one another, children tucked under arms, elders carried in makeshift stretchers. They come clutching sacks of bread, blankets, family heirlooms. I imagine they brought what they thought would be most important. Some carry nothing at all, their hands open and shaking as if they already know they've lost everything.

We have set up a stronghold here, within the castle walls, but it is a stopgap at best. The true border, the one that once encircled all of Altinna and kept it safe for centuries, is holding for now, but it is splintering. I can feel it every time I pass near it, every time I reach with my senses toward the fragile threads of magic that once thrummed confidently through the land. That barrier is a dying creature, hissing with every breath, waiting for the moment it can finally draw its last breath.

Beyond it, the Oceanans and Ambrosians have made camp. I cannot see them from where I stand now, but I know they are out there, waiting and watching, ready to strike the instant they're all back on their feet.

But I can see none of what they have planned. The moment Akin disappeared into the dark shadows, my Sight disappeared with him. I press my fingertips hard into my temples, digging into the space between bone and skin as though pressure alone could restore the Sight that has always been my guide. My breath is shallow. The world swims behind my eyes, but not with vision, only fatigue, frustration, and the spinning dread of helplessness.

I see nothing. There are no glimpses of futures, no flickers of alternate paths. There are not even shadows of what could be. There is only the heavy, aching darkness behind my eyes, the silence of a gift that once spoke constantly but now says nothing at all. It fractured the moment Akin fell.

That moment replays over and over again in my mind like a punishment. I try not to think about it, but my memory drags me back every time I close my eyes. Akin turning, blood soaking through his side, his legs folding. Then came the shadows. They were unnatural, silent, and insatiable. They claimed him, removed his body from this realm before I could reach him. And I saw none of it coming, even though I should have.

I have never missed something like that before. I have always known when danger was near, when threads of time were splitting in ways they should not. I've always had a warning. But not this time. The Sight failed me. Or maybe I failed it. Either way, he is gone, and I was blind. And now I am blind to the future.

Without my Sight, who am I? It's all I've had to offer throughout my life. It's allowed me to rise to the ranks, to become a trusted advisor of a queen in a foreign land. Without it, I'm just another fae with nothing useful to offer. What can I give to Maerilee now? I always assumed I was chosen to be hers because of my Sight, and now there is nothing.

I glance toward her now, seated at the far edge of the hall beside her mother. She is wrapped in a thick cloak, her arms drawn tightly across her chest, her eyes fixed on nothing. She hasn't spoken since the smaller barrier was raised. She nods when spoken to. She moves when guided. But she is not here, not really. She is somewhere deep inside herself, curled around a grief so consuming it has hollowed her out.

And I cannot help her. I can't even help myself.

Brook is nearby, not far from the doors that lead out to the courtyard. He leans against the wall, pale and drawn, his chest still bound in thick wrappings from the stab wound that nearly ended him. He hasn't said much either, but I can see in his eyes that he is thinking. Always thinking. Always reaching for understanding. He is watching Maerilee like she is the center of every truth he has left.

River, on the other hand, burns. He is full of an anger and rage that the rest of us can't quite access yet. He is restless and dangerous, with nothing productive to channel all that emotion into. He paces the corridor, back and forth, his jaw locked and shoulders tight. Every few minutes he stops just long enough to clench his fists and stare at the walls like he wishes he could bring them down. There is fury in him now. I do not know if it is for Akin, or for the army waiting to destroy us, or for himself. Maybe it is all three.

None of us are doing well, all so consumed with grief and hopelessness. And I have no way to guide us back.

I try again to summon a vision, closing my eyes, reaching for the lines of possibility I have followed since I was young. I expect resistance, but I do not even find that. There is nothing to push against. Only emptiness. The threads are gone. The map is gone. I am walking without direction, and there is no light in the distance. I open my eyes again and let out a slow breath, tasting the bitterness of failure on my tongue.

I finally force myself outside, to a balcony where I can see over the horizon. The barrier still glows faintly beyond the courtyard. I can feel the strain of it in the air. It is holding for now, but we all know it will not hold forever. A single break is all it will take, and we have no plan for what happens when that break comes.

A FUTURE KING

I can't take the silence anymore. Grief fills every hallway, every breath, every conversation that ends before it begins. Akin's death has carved a hollow space inside each of us, and even though no one says his name out loud, it echoes through the palace like a ghost.

It's been two days since his death, and the silence threatens to crush me. It presses too close, sits too heavy on my shoulders. I need to move. I need to do something, anything, other than sit in that war room listening to generals argue over plans they can't agree on. Outside of the room is no better, though.

Maerilee has completely shut down, unable to function since she erected the barrier around the castle. Grief has stolen more from her than anyone. Permiton is likewise pretending he isn't unraveling, but something is wrong with him. He's barely spoken since Akin's death, but unlike Maerilee, he seems more agitated than anything. Brook is still recovering, barely able to stay upright, despite the Bright Waters.

We are a rudderless ship without Akin. I never expected to feel so lost without one of the Four. I'd assumed Maerilee needed us and we needed Maerilee, but I didn't understand that we needed each other too. Without Akin, we are fractured. I'm not sure that we'll ever be whole again, and I don't know what that means for any of us. I hate not knowing things.

I walk through the corridors of the castle with no destination. I don't really need one. I just need air that hasn't been laced with grief, a room that isn't suffocating with indecision and confusion. But there's nowhere to go. Only the soldiers are allowed to leave the barrier of the castle, and that's only for quick errands. If the kingdom's barrier falls while they're outside of the castle's barrier, they could be lost forever.

But gods, the castle is so damn crowded. There are far too many people, and not enough space. The hallways are lined with makeshift bedding, rations being counted out, guards taking up posts in corners they never used to stand in. The refugees from the kingdom fill every empty space, all afraid and unsure of what to do with themselves. Some sit in silence. Others murmur to one another in hushed voices, not wanting to draw attention, not wanting to break the fragile illusion of safety.

I pass a mother with her arms around three small children, their eyes wide and red-rimmed, all curled into her skirts like they're afraid she'll vanish if they let go. Further down, a man holds the hand of a woman who can't stop shaking, rocking slightly with her eyes fixed on nothing.

The battle may have paused, but the war is still here. It's in the way people breathe, the way they flinch at every loud sound, the way they clutch their meager possessions like they'll be taken away at any second. It's in the smoke that drifts through the cracked windows, curling under doors from the fires still smoldering beyond the barrier. It's in the silence that follows the sobs when someone runs out of tears. And yet, there's an endurance about all of them, a firm belief that they will be okay at the end of this.

I was raised to believe Altinna was weaker than Oceana. It was said like a fact, like a truth that needed no evidence. We were told they were soft, too reliant on their queens and old magic, too wrapped up in art and beauty to be taken seriously. I believed it. I never questioned it. Even when I first came here, I held on to that assumption like a shield. If they were weaker, it would excuse my own failures. If they were weaker, it meant I didn't have to look too closely at how strong they truly were.

But looking at them now, huddled in these narrow corridors with nothing but fear and resolve to keep them upright, I realize how wrong I was. These people are not weak. They are surviving. And that kind of strength does not come from power or privilege. It comes from something older. Something deeper. Something I don't think I understood until today.

I turn a corner and stop abruptly when I see a group of children pressed against the far wall. There are five of them, ranging in age from infancy to maybe nine or ten. They're quiet, but their eyes are huge, following every movement, alert in the way only frightened children are. Two of them cling to each other, and one is chewing on the edge of his sleeve like it's the only thing keeping him from falling apart. The oldest looking girl clutches the baby to her, and I can't help but wonder where their parents are.

A palace servant rushes by, her arms full of bread and dried fruit. She's trying to move quickly, her face lined with exhaustion and tension. The basket looks too heavy for her, but she doesn't slow. She's moving toward the families a little further down, trying to make sure the food gets where it's needed.

Before I can think, I step forward to help her. She blinks up at me in surprise, almost startled enough to drop the basket. Her eyes flick from my face to the insignia on my chest, to the sword at my hip, and then back again.

"Pardon me, Your Highness," she says in a thick Altinnian accent. "I'm just trying to get these people fed."

"I can take that," I say simply, reaching for the basket.

She doesn't move at first, watching me warily.

"Please," I say, almost desperately. "I just want to help."

She finally nods slowly and lets me lift the weight from her arms. Her hands fall to her sides, visibly trembling. She gives me a grateful nod before stepping back and disappearing into the crowd, probably to get more food.

The basket is heavier than I expected, but I carry it toward the children, crouching low so I don't tower over them. Their eyes follow me the whole way, wary and cautious, their bodies tense like they expect the food to be snatched away at any second. I kneel beside them and speak softly.

"Hi, there," I say as gently as I can. I don't have much experience with children. "Are you hungry?"

They say nothing, but one of the smaller girls nods once. Her lip is trembling, and her fingers are white-knuckled where she clings to her older brother's sleeve.

I pull out a small piece of bread and hold it out to her. She doesn't take it right away. Her eyes dart between the food and my face, like she's trying to decide if I'm dangerous or if she can trust me. After a long pause, she reaches out and takes it gently, holding it to her chest like it's made of gold.

The others follow, slowly, cautiously, each accepting a bit of fruit or bread or nuts. The baby is handed a hunk of bread to gum on. They don't smile. They don't speak. But they eat, and something in my chest tightens so hard I have to look away.

This is what we're fighting for. Not pride. Not politics. Not thrones or borders or the egos of men who will never know these children's names. We're fighting for these kids. For their safety and their future. For the chance that one day they won't flinch when someone raises their voice, or tremble when someone drops a cup too loudly.

I hand out the rest of the food slowly, one piece at a time, making sure each of them gets something, even though I know it won't be enough to keep them full. But it is something. A moment of kindness. A small thread of humanity pulled from the wreckage of everything else.

One of the boys looks up at me, crumbs on his chin, and whispers something so soft I almost don't hear it.

"Thank you," he says with all the manners he can muster.

I swallow hard, my throat tight with emotion, and nod.

"You're welcome," I tell him earnestly.

I rise slowly and leave the empty basket by the wall. As I walk back through the corridors, the weight in my chest hasn't disappeared, but it feels different now. Heavier in some places, lighter in others. I still don't know what we'll do when the barrier falls. I don't know how we'll hold the line. I don't know how to fill the void Akin left behind.

But I do know this. I will fight for these people. Not because I have to, but because they are worth fighting for.

Altinna is not my kingdom. Its halls were not built for me, its people did not ask for me, and the woman I fight for is not mine to claim, but none of that matters now. Even if I don't belong here, I am here. And right now, these people are terrified, and they need more than magic and orders to make it through the day. They need to see that someone is still paying attention. That someone sees them.

So I keep walking, looking for more hungry people and scared children. I move through the castle, pausing at every hallway, every stairwell, every crammed room that has been repurposed into a makeshift shelter. I stop and speak softly with the families huddled together, offering what little reassurance I can. I carry water jugs where they need to go. I lift baskets too heavy for the servants to carry. I make sure the soldiers on rotation get their share of bread before it is handed out again.

It is not enough. I know that. But it is something.

It is strange, the feeling that settles in my chest as I move through the palace. I've never served anyone other than myself, not really. I have worn the title of prince, have commanded with authority I never earned, have taken and spoken and postured as if the world owed me something. But here, stripped of that arrogance and title, I feel something different.

I feel useful.

I'm not sure when that began to matter to me, but it feels like the only thing left in the world.

At some point, I find myself back near the central staircase. The halls are thinner here, the ceiling lower. I hear voices ahead, a familiar one among them. King Fratino stands near the inner gate, speaking quietly to a few of his guards. He sees me before I have the chance to turn away. His eyes follow me, and after a beat, he lifts one hand to dismiss the men beside him. They nod and move away, leaving the two of us alone.

I consider walking the other way, but I don't. Instead, I approach. He watches me in silence as I stop a few feet away. For a moment, neither of us speaks. He studies me with the same calculating expression he wore when my family first arrived to Altinna for Maerilee's ball.

He didn't trust me then, and he was right not to. It's only been a few weeks, but it feels like a lifetime ago. I was a different person, someone who only cared about status and power. I wanted to be Maerilee's One so we could secure a powerful alliance with Altinna and both of our kingdoms could experience more power and wealth. I felt entitled to her then.

But our journey changed me. The war has changed me. Hell, the last few hours have changed me. I don't feel entitled to anything anymore. I don't feel like a prince or a leader at all. I'm just as scared as everyone else, and it's my fault all of this is happening.

"You have been walking the castle for hours," King Fratino says by way of greeting.

I shrug.

"It's far better than sitting still," I admit. "It's nice to feel useful."

He tilts his head slightly.

"I thought you were the kind of man who preferred to be waited on, not one who handed out bread to children."

His tone is not mocking or cruel. He's being entirely sincere. And he isn't remotely wrong.

I meet his gaze without flinching.

"I used to be," I tell him honestly, unable to verbalize exactly what changed.

He studies me again. Then, slowly, he steps forward and clasps his hands behind his back. His voice is quieter now, the edge softened.

"My wife and I do not always agree," he says. "But I have always admired her devotion to our people. Even when it exhausted her. Even when it cost her more than anyone saw. She believes in duty. In care. In doing the work, even when no one is watching."

He pauses, then looks at me again.

"I saw you give rations to a child today. I saw you lift a wounded man you didn't know. That's not the prince I expected you to be."

I say nothing, unsure what I'm supposed to feel under the weight of his words.

"You may not be from this kingdom," he continues, "but the people are beginning to see you. That matters."

I shake my head slightly, the words catching in my throat.

"I don't know what I'm doing. Not really."

"No one does," he replies. "Especially not the ones who pretend they do."

His eyes drift toward the courtyard beyond the gate. The barrier still glows faintly beyond it, though it flickers at the edges now, fading in and out like a breath that grows shorter with time.

"I don't know how this will end," he says softly. "I don't know if we'll survive. But I do know this. The true sign of a good leader is not how loudly he commands or how many men bow when he enters a room. It is how willing he is to serve the weakest in his kingdom. To bend, when others expect him to stand tall. To kneel, when others only know how to climb."

I don't respond right away. The words land with more weight than I expect. All my life, I thought strength meant being above others, and being seen. Being feared. But everything I thought I knew has unraveled. As I stare into his eyes, I realize I don't want to go back to the man I was. I want to be who he sees.

King Fratino turns toward me again and lays a hand briefly on my shoulder.

"You may not see it yet," he says. "But I think you will be a strong leader, River. Not because of who you were born to be. But because of who you choose to become."

Before I can say anything, one of the generals approaches at a brisk pace.

"Your Majesty," he says, bowing quickly. "Apologies for the interruption. A war meeting has been called. The Queen is already in the council room."

The king nods once, then looks back at me.

"You should be there too."

"Yes, Your Majesty."

He gives me a final nod and follows the general down the corridor.

I remain where I am for a moment longer, my hands curled into loose fists, my breath steadying. This isn't my kingdom by birth. But that doesn't mean I don't belong here. Maybe belonging is something to be earned.

CHANGING THE TIDE

Brook

I stand at the table in the middle of the war room, the edges of the massive map curling up slightly under my palms, and listen as the generals argue around me. Their voices are low and tense, an overlapping hum of uncertainty and exhaustion that fills the space. At least they aren't yelling at each other anymore. No one has the energy for that left in them. Instead, they speak in clipped phrases, drawing lines and circles on the map trying to find the best approach to end this war, like any of this can still be planned.

Maerilee is a shell of herself now. She sits at the head of the table, a heavy cloak pulled tight around her shoulders, her eyes glassy and distant. Her hands stay folded in her lap. Her mouth never moves. She's still breathing, but only barely. It's like I can feel her grief in my own body. I wish I could carry it for her. Her people need her far more than they need me.

River enters the room not far behind the king. I don't know where he's been all day, but I realize it's the first time I've seen him. He looks more weary than I've ever known him to be. We haven't spoken since

I almost died. I haven't even had a chance to thank him for saving my life. Knowing him, he'll probably just brush it off and say it was his job or something stupid like that. He's so stubborn.

Permiton is crouched in a corner staring into the distance. He whispers words to himself that no one else can hear, so we've all just left him alone. I'm sure the generals would prefer that all of us just leave them to it. None of us are of any use to them now. But I can't tear myself away from this room. With Akin gone, there's no one to stand in for us, to represent us as the future Kings of Altinna.

My ribs still ache, but the pain is dull and manageable now. It reminds me that, unlike Akin, I survived. I shouldn't have, and I know it. If it weren't for River's quick thinking, and his sacrifice of leaving the battlefield, I probably would have bled out instantly. But now I'm here, and Akin isn't. Would he have had a chance if River had stayed on that field?

I try to push the thought aside. What-ifs will drive me crazy until the day I die. The important thing is that I am here now and I have to do him proud. He always protected Maerilee with his life. He always put her first, above anyone else. With Permiton falling apart and River lost to his anger and agitation, that leaves Maerilee's wellbeing to me. I can't fail her. I can't fail Akin.

The generals talk about formations and fallback positions and the strength of the barrier, but none of it sounds like it will work. They're stalling, the same way we all are, because no one wants to be the first to say what we're all thinking. We're not strong enough to hold the line if the Oceanans attack again. We were barely strong enough before, and we took several massive blows.

Losing Akin isn't nearly as significant to the generals as it was to the four of us. He was Maerilee's personal guard, not an active soldier, not a field commander with troops under his control. His death didn't fracture the structure of our defense the way losing a captain might have.

But many others died on that battlefield as well. The ranks have shrunk from the small size they already were. Another battle would leave us decimated. No one can seem to outthink that particular problem.

One of the generals across from me clears his throat and leans forward.

"The scouts report movement along the northern ridge," he says. "We believe they're setting up artillery just outside of range. They're testing the barrier."

"We won't hold if they strike from two fronts," another general adds, his voice tight. "The army is too scattered, and the reserves we called for haven't arrived. We've lost too many."

"We haven't lost everyone," I say, and the sound of my voice surprises even me.

They all turn to look at me.

I keep my hands on the table, keep my breath steady. I'm not used to speaking in this room, not used to having my words carry any weight. But my brain is the one thing I can still rely on, and I'm going to use it.

"We may not be at full strength," I continue. "But the Oceanans don't know that. Not really. Maerilee knocked them out. They have no idea how large of a loss we've suffered. They're only testing the barrier because they're still trying to figure out how much damage we took. If we let them keep thinking we're broken, they'll hit us the moment it cracks."

"Are you suggesting we bluff?" the general asks.

"I'm suggesting we make it look like we're stronger than we are. They think we'll be scattered. That we'll hesitate. That we'll fall back and try to protect too many points at once until we stretch ourselves too thin. That's their strategy. It always has been."

My fingers skim the edge of the map, and I study it for a moment until I'm able to trace a place I know the army will attack.

"They'll strike here first," I tap the point where the terrain dips near the eastern ridge, where the barrier flickers the most. "It's the weakest point in the barrier's coverage. They've already sent scouts in that direction. They'll aim to force us to divide our forces to defend this gap, which leaves the western wall vulnerable. They won't stop with one breach. They'll open as many as they can and bleed us out."

Someone exhales behind me. It sounds like a grunt of doubt, but no one speaks over me.

I straighten, letting my shoulders square as I look around the table. They still don't trust me. That's clear in the lines of their faces, in the way their eyes dart toward Queen Kimalissa or King Fratino as though waiting for someone else to vouch for me. I'm the former prince of their enemy kingdom, and not the crown prince at that.

But finally, my reading is paying off. I've studied every military training book that Oceana has ever produced. I've read the ancient record of our wars and studied the strategies that have been passed down over the ages. I know Commander Heela's playbook better than he does.

"So we don't let them," I go on. "We don't react. We don't chase them from breach to breach. We hold. We force them into a battle they can't sustain. We make them come to us."

The generals all stare at me before they start murmuring amongst themselves. Some of the men shift uncomfortably. One of them, the older one with the jagged scar along his jawline, crosses his arms and looks me up and down like he's trying to place me. I recognize him as General Areson. He's tussled with Oceanan rebels in the past.

"You speak with confidence, Prince Brook," he says. "But what experience do you have in war?"

My jaw tightens, but I don't let the words sting.

"I was never a soldier," I reply. "But I studied every campaign Oceana ever launched. I spent my life reading about the battles, the terrain, the tactics our generals used and misused. I know how they think. I know how my father thinks. And more importantly, I know what they expect us to do."

"And you suggest we ignore the breaches?" another general interjects, this one younger, sharper, his voice laced with skepticism. "Let them tear through the weak points while we wait?"

"No," I say. "I'm saying we make the weak points look like traps. We prepare fallback positions they don't see coming. We guide them into kill zones. If they want us to break, then we show them we already know where they're going and that we've been waiting for them there."

The room stills again. And then, slowly, someone clears their throat.

"I've seen it done," General Greson says after a long beat. "During the last skirmish nearly a century ago, we turned the river valley near Westden into a death field. We lured the Oceanans in with a staged retreat, then hit them from both sides."

There's a murmur of agreement. One of the mapmakers nods and starts sketching on the edge of the parchment. And still, Maerilee says nothing.

She hasn't lifted her eyes from the table, hasn't acknowledged any of this. She is a statue, and I don't know whether she's listening or drifting further from us with every breath. I want her to look at me, even if just once. I want her to see me now, standing steady, trying to carry a piece of this burden she thinks she has to carry alone.

But it's not her voice I hear next. It's the Queen's.

"We will proceed with Prince Brook's strategy."

Her voice is clear, strong, and final. All the murmurs die instantly. Queen Kimalissa rises from her place at the head of the table, her gaze sweeping the room with quiet authority. She looks every inch a ruler, even if her magic has not returned. Her power was never in spells or sigils. It was in the way she commands a room, even through grief.

"I trust his knowledge," she says. "And I trust his instinct. He has given up his country and his family, and now he fights at our side. That isn't an easy burden to carry, but he wears it well. He almost lost his life on the battlefield, but here he stands giving us the best strategy I've heard all day. We go with his plan."

She turns to look at me, and in that moment, I feel something settle inside me. A knot of doubt I have carried for years loosens, just a little. My spine straightens. My chest expands.

They are listening to me. Not because of River. Not because I'm royalty. Not because I'm standing in the right room. Because I know what I'm talking about.

One by one, the generals begin to nod. They shift from skeptical to committed. Orders begin to be passed. Positions adjusted. I watch as my words become action, become strategy, become real.

I look up to see River watching me in amazement. He doesn't look annoyed or frustrated. He doesn't look jealous that I'm being respected. He actually looks proud of me. I'm not entirely sure what to do with that. It's not a reaction I'm used to from him.

When I turn to Maerilee, though, she has not moved. She gives no indication that she's even aware there are war plans happening around her. She is a broken husk of who she once was, and I'm terrified for her.

COMFORT IN THE CHAOS

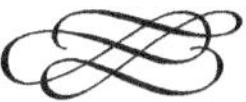

I SIT BY THE WINDOW OF MY CHAMBERS, THE STONE SEAT BENEATH ME chilled despite the fire burning low behind me. Outside, my kingdom glows orange and gold with the fires still burning from our enemies. Smoke rises into the sky, making it nearly impossible to tell if it's night or day. Not that I've been paying much attention anyway. Time means nothing anymore.

Akin may have died days ago, or seconds for all I know. There's no telling how long it's been, I just know that there is a definite split in time. Before Akin died, everything made sense. After, everything crumbled into ash. I know I can't let this grief swallow me. I know that I have to show up for my people and for myself. But it feels like there's nothing left to live for, and that alone keeps me glued to this bench, staring aimlessly at my kingdom on fire.

There's some hope, though. Where I've faltered, Brook stood up and took charge. He gave the army a strategy to hold onto. When I'm able to focus, I hear about their small victories. They've been dividing and conquering our enemies exquisitely. And yet, I cannot make myself be happy about them.

Everything about this is tenuous. The barrier remains intact, but it flickers more now than ever. The longer this battle rages, the more it will weaken, and then we may be lost. The barrier around the castle is strong for now, but a castle is not a kingdom. It is a fort, a stronghold, a last desperate hope. The people are already frightened and weary, and there's no comfort I can bring them.

I close my eyes and lean my forehead against the glass pane, though it's cold enough to sting. I welcome it. At least it's a feeling. It's a small light shining through the endless darkness of my pain.

I constantly feel the ache of everything I cannot fix. I can't heal the barrier. I can't bring back Akin. I can't restore my mother's magic. I don't know how to hold my people together when I'm crumbling in the dark. I am a queen of shadows, and nothing else. Our kingdom is doomed because of me.

My family has had to step in to cover for my absence. My Four… my Three… have found ways to be useful to the kingdom where I have failed. They are holding us together, holding the kingdom together. I should be grateful. I am.

I just don't know how to hold myself together anymore.

The barrier won't last forever. We all know it. And when it falls, our enemies will come like a tsunami, consuming everything in their wake. I don't know what they'll do to my people. They may enslave them or imprison them. They may kill them if they're generous. All will certainly be lost and Altinna will fall.

I lift my gaze again, watching the flicker of torchlight along the outer wall. There are soldiers stationed there now, marching between towers, keeping vigil even though they are half-starved and covered in the dirt and sweat of days without proper rest. They fight anyway. They stand anyway. They still look toward the horizon with their hands on their swords, hoping that help will come.

I envy them for their conviction. I believe in nothing anymore. I have no hope left. I have no future to fight for. All is already lost, and the loss consumes me like the shadows that stole Akin away from me. What do I fight for now that he's gone?

A knock sounds faintly against the outer door. I don't answer, but a moment later, it opens anyway. Brook steps inside. His shoulders are stiff, and his posture tense. He hesitates when he sees me by the window, like he isn't sure if he's welcome. But then he comes forward, slowly, until he stands just beside me. For a while, we don't speak.

It's been like this, for however long I've been lost to the shadows. He comes to me periodically, telling me about military operations, though I can only pretend to care.

"They hit the northern slope again," he says eventually. His voice is low. "We were ready for them this time. The trap worked."

I nod without looking at him, without responding. He must have anticipated this, because he keeps going without any encouragement from me.

"We didn't sustain any losses," he says. "It's like a miracle. We're finally gaining some ground in this gods-forsaken war. As long as the Oceanans continue to spread out like this, we have a fighting chance."

I nod again.

He doesn't leave. Instead, he shifts to lean his shoulder lightly against the wall, his gaze following mine toward the fires flickering in the distance.

"They're afraid, Maerilee," he says after another long moment. "The people. The soldiers. But they haven't lost hope. Not yet."

"That must feel nice," I say, swiping at a falling tear. "I would kill to find my hope again."

"You don't have to," he says gently, sitting down across from me and taking my hand in both of his. "I will hope for you, Maerilee. I will carry your burden. Just tell me what you need."

I look at him then, really look at him, and I see a change in him. Gods, how long has it been since this war started? He seems to be so different now, so much more confident than when we first met. He's not a spare prince lost in his brother's shadow anymore. He has purpose, command. He's strong in every way that I am weak, and I realize how desperately I would love to rest against his shoulder and try to soak up some of that strength.

"I'm glad you're here," I say softly, shifting so that I'm lying against his chest. He wraps his arms around me, and I feel his breath tickle the top of my head.

"I'm not going anywhere," he murmurs into my hair. "You have to know, no matter how hard things get, I'm always going to be here for you, Maerilee. You don't have to hope for that or wish for it. That's just fact."

"You've changed," I whisper.

He looks down at me, surprised, but he doesn't deny it.

"We've all changed," he finally mutters, "in good ways and bad."

I pull away, looking up at him, and finding nothing but kindness and affection in his eyes.

"Do you think I'm broken, Brook?" I ask, suddenly terrified of what his answer will be.

I know I am. I've shattered completely. If I looked into a mirror now, I wouldn't recognize myself. My soul has fractured since Akin's death, but there are other parts of my soul that have to keep surviving. One part of my soul belongs to Brook.

He shakes his head and begins stroking my hair in a comforting gesture.

"You're surviving the best way you can," he says, and this time his voice is firm. "You think that's nothing, but it isn't. You think you're broken, but you aren't. You're grieving, and it will take time."

"We don't have time," I sob, snuggling back into his chest. "You would all be better without me holding you back."

The tears catch me off guard. I've cried so much I thought I didn't have anything left, but the admission forces them out of me. And his steadfastness, the way he holds me tightly without comment or need to correct me, makes me feel safe enough to let it all out.

"I don't know how to move forward," I confess. "I don't know how to do this without him."

I feel him sigh into my hair, feel his chest move up and down as he processes my words. He continues to be strong. He continues to be brave. How can he do it? How does he go on when the world feels like it's ending?

"You're not doing it alone," he says softly. "We are all hurting from this, Maerilee. We're all grieving in our own ways. Akin became like a brother to me, and I'm devastated by the loss. I know it's different for me. I didn't love him in the same way you loved him. But I love you, and I will never stop fighting to save you."

My whole body shakes with the force of my sobs. How can he love me when I'm so useless? I think I've forgotten how to love myself. I think I've forgotten how to love. Yet somewhere, deep inside of me, there is a burning love for Brook. For so long, it was a protective love, a need to show River and his parents that Brook was just as worthy of love as they were. Now he's returning that love ten times over, and I don't feel worthy of it.

"I'm scared," I whisper.

"Me too," he admits, surprising me.

He continues to fight through his fear. He's so strong and brave, so resilient in the face of our doom.

We sit there for a long time, the world quiet around us, the war momentarily distant. His hand strokes up and down my back, slow and soothing. His heart beats steady beneath my cheek.

I tilt my head to look at him, and our eyes meet.

There's no rush. No urgency. Just a quiet understanding, an ache that lives in both of us. We don't kiss immediately. We just look at each other, like we're still figuring out if this is allowed, if it's okay to want something gentle in the middle of so much ruin.

But then I reach for him. And he meets me halfway.

The kiss is soft. Tender. His lips brush mine with care, not hunger, like he's afraid I'll break. And maybe I will, but I know that he'll be there to put me back together

We move slowly, hands exploring carefully, reverently. He removes his tunic, and I fumble with the button of my dress. There's no desperation in it. No need to escape. Just the need to feel something other than pain. The need to remind ourselves that we're still alive, still capable of connection, of warmth, of something real.

When he lifts me into his arms and carries me to the bed, he does it like I'm something precious. And when he lays me down and joins me there, he never stops looking at me. Not once. He leaves hot, warm kisses on every inch of my exposed skin, whispering words that are so tender and beautiful, I feel like I'll break apart under them.

"You're beautiful," he says.

"You're strong."

"I love you."

"I'm here for you."

"I need you."

I can't speak, so I just feel. It's just another flicker of something good in the hollowness, and I know that it's fleeting. The moment he's gone, I will feel like a shell of myself again. But that's a problem for later. For now, I wind my hands around his waist, cling to his shoulders, find purchase wherever I can. He is the only thing tethering me to this world now, so I can't let go.

He kisses at the hollow under my ear, nips at the tender spot on my neck just below. I close my eyes and let myself forget, just for a moment, that there's any pain in this world. He brings me only pleasure, only love.

"You are so amazing," he whispers against my collarbone, before once again capturing my lips in his.

I love the way he feels on top of me. It makes me feel weighed down after feeling so weightless for so long. I was drifting through the air with no place to land, but now I am safe on the ground, held together by his touch.

Then he slides a finger between my wet folds, lighting a fire inside me that rivals anything burning outside. I gasp at the touch, encouraging so much more. I need to feel every inch of him, of his fingers, his mouth, his manhood. My body and mind are no more than desire now, I've transformed into want and need, nothing more, and nothing less.

Something in me whispers that I'm being selfish, that I shouldn't be allowed to feel so much warmth and love when there is a war waging. But then his fingers are doing wicked things, forcing me up and up and up, and then I'm weightless again, but in a totally different way. I cling to him as a powerful wave of pleasure crashes over me, and it makes me feel less alone. Maybe I won't drift away, as long as I have him here with me.

"I want more," I whisper in a lustful voice I don't even recognize. "I need you, Brook. More than I've ever needed anyone or anything."

"Are you sure?" he asks, his voice barely a whisper.

"Yes," I breathe.

He kisses me again, his tongue battling mine for control. I thread my fingers through his hair, anchor myself to him as he moves above me. When he enters me, I feel like I might explode into stars, still so sensitive from the bliss he just brought me.

Our bodies find a rhythm easily, slow and delicate, but still full of want and need. Each of his gasps, his moans of pleasure, bring me closer and closer to my own. If I can't do anything else for my people, I can at least still bring him pleasure. I can still show him how much I love him, even if my words fail.

As we come undone together, clinging to each other as we fall over the edge of pleasure, the world falls away. For the first time in days, I feel something other than sorrow. It doesn't erase the grief. Nothing could. But it reminds me that I am still here. That I am still capable of feeling joy, of sharing it, even in the smallest way.

When we finish, we stay tangled together in my sheets, skin to skin, breath to breath.

"I'm not going to let you fall apart," Brook whispers in my ear, his voice rough and fierce and full of quiet resolve. "I don't care what happens next. We're going to make it through this. All of us."

I bury my face against his neck and try to believe his promise.

AN UNEXPECTED VISION

It's been two weeks since the first clash beyond the barrier, and somehow life inside the castle has adjusted to the rhythm of siege and skirmish. Every morning begins with patrol updates and casualty reports. Every evening ends with silence and smoke. And in between, we've found some sense of normalcy. The people of the kingdom have transformed from terrified refugees to a brave community.

Walking through the crowded halls no longer feels like walking through a graveyard. The people have come back to life in unexpected ways, turning their fear into action. They help in the kitchens, create gifts for the soldiers, tell stories and grow closer than they ever have. While I wasn't in this kingdom long before the war, I know that there's a closeness amongst the people that didn't exist before. They aren't just neighbors anymore. They've become something of a family.

It's equal parts encouraging and unsettling. Then again, everything unsettles me lately. For instance, River has become something of a mentor to the children in the kingdom. Every time I catch a glimpse of him, he's either huddled with a group of children, telling them some story he learned in Oceana, or he's teaching them a game. The children squeal with laughter, and the love they have for him is undeniable. The relieved looks on their parents' faces is also uplifting.

Yet that isn't who I've known River to be, nor is it who I thought he would become. Though it's true, I didn't spend much time looking into his future, this isn't a path I foresaw for him. He's opened his heart in an unexpected way. He's changed his own destiny.

There's a warmth to him now that wasn't there before, and it's genuine enough to confuse me. It's not performative, not for Maerilee or the court. It's as if something in him cracked open, and what spilled out was good. It makes no sense.

Brook, on the other hand, has become a general in all but title. He no longer lingers at the edge of conversations. He stands at the center of them now, gesturing to maps, discussing flanking positions, negotiating troop movements. The others listen to him. They defer to him. I watch him from a distance sometimes, wondering when he stopped being quiet and brooding and became a true leader.

They've both evolved in unexpected ways, and it scares me. If they can change their fates, what else is possible? I'd love to believe that this war could end in our favor, but I have no way of knowing anymore. I have lost my ability to see the future, and each passing day makes it more apparent and more terrifying.

At first, I thought it was just the grief. The weight of Akin's death hit me harder than I thought it would. But now I wonder if something deeper was lost in that moment, like a thread was severed, and I don't know how to reweave it.

So I spend my days buried in the royal library, chasing ghosts in ink. The room has become my cell and my sanctuary. The air smells like paper, dust, and something faintly medicinal from the poultices stored behind the cabinets. I've read everything on prophetic magic, on Sight, on the strain of loss. Admittedly, there's very little to be learned. There are plenty of prophecies, but what used to make sense to me now sounds like jumbled nonsense.

Nothing speaks to the loss of Sight. Either it's never happened, or no one has ever written about it. This gift is rare as it is, so I shouldn't be surprised. But it makes it no less frustrating. Without my vision, I can't contribute anything. Sure, I still have my magic, but even that feels weak and fractured.

I haven't spoken to Maerilee in days. I see her sometimes, usually seated by a window, her face pale, eyes hollow. I haven't gone to her. I don't know what to say to her or how to comfort her when I have no words of comfort to give. Before, I could tell her what would happen next. I could assure her that the future showed our favor. Not anymore. Now I can only give her false promises, and I refuse to do that to her. I refuse to give her unsubstantiated hope that could be snatched away at any moment.

Tonight, the lamps are low in the library. I've been here the entire day, barely leaving to eat. I haven't said a single word to anyone, and phlegm has gathered in my throat from disuse. The sun has set. The halls are quiet. I sit in a worn velvet chair beside the last of the firelight, an open book in my lap that I stopped reading several pages ago.

My head aches, and my bones feel weary. I close my eyes for just a moment, hoping to find some relief in the darkness. When I open them again, the firelight is gone.

The world around me is not the library. It is nothing. There is no other way to describe it. I am in a dark pit of nothingness, space made of shadow and silence, cold and endless. The darkness is so dense it feels like it's inside of me, consuming me too. My heart stutters in my chest, and I try to move, but my limbs feel heavy and sluggish.

I try to tell myself that I'm only dreaming, that I can snap myself out of this at any time, but it doesn't feel like a dream. It doesn't feel like a vision either, though. My visions always come with clarity, with the intense knowledge that what I'm witnessing will come to pass in some distant or not-so-distant future.

This is something else entirely. It's hazy, slipping at the edges. And besides all that, I don't dream. I never have. Seers don't dream. Our minds are so lost to the future, sleep is our only time to experience peace. It is our payment for the very real sacrifice we have to make by tapping into the Sight.

Something is very, very wrong here. Shapes flicker in the distance and I try to catch them. I step forward, uncertain, my boots making no sound on the nonexistent floor. The shadows part and a sound rises. Not a voice, but a cry of pain, sudden, piercing, and blinding.

I drop to my knees with a gasp, my hands clutching at my chest. It feels like a blade has been driven straight through me, but when I look down, there is no wound and no blood. Yet I feel it all the same.

I realize then that it's not my pain. It's someone else's. I breathe through it, shaking, struggling to push to my feet. The moment I rise, I see a figure lying on the ground. I recognize him instantly, as I've replayed the moment over and over in my head since the moment he fell.

It's Akin.

He's curled into himself, cloaked in shadow, but it's unmistakably him. His shoulders are broad, his posture somehow proud, even in the midst of unimaginable pain. It's the way I saw him in his last moments, and I begin to wonder if this is just a memory. I approach him, expecting him to be whisked away again into the shadows, but he remains visible as I get closer.

As I approach, I realize his body is surrounded by tendrils of darkness, wrapped around him like chains. They writhe around him, tightening, binding. His arms are limp at his sides. He isn't moving. I can't even tell if he's breathing.

I stagger toward him.

"Akin," I whisper, my voice echoing strangely in the space. "Akin, can you hear me?"

He doesn't respond. He's bound in darkness. He is literally chained in shadow.

His eyes eventually open, slowly, and they find mine. It feels like the breath is stolen from my lungs. He looks at me like he's trying to anchor himself, like I am the last thing keeping him from dissolving completely. His mouth opens, and though no sound escapes, I hear him all the same.

Help me.

The words don't echo in the air. They don't come from his lips.

They rip through my mind like a shard of glass, sharp and unmistakable.

"I'm trying," I whisper. "I'm trying, Akin."

The darkness thickens. It curls around my legs, pulls at my arms, crawls across my chest, relentless. It wants to consume me too, to obscure me from sight. Maybe it's the thing obscuring my Sight. And I understand, in a way I can't explain, that this magic was meant to hide him. To bury him in a place no one could find.

But I've found him, even if I can't get to him.

Akin shudders. His image flickers. One moment he's solid, struggling against the shadow. The next he's translucent, as though he's made of light that's losing its anchor to the world. I lurch forward again, forcing my body through whatever is holding me, but my hands pass through his arm like mist.

"No," I choke out. "Stay with me. Please."

His lips form my name, and for a moment, I see something change in his expression. Hope flickers across his face. Then the void explodes in white light. I jolt awake.

I'm back in the library, exactly where my body has been this entire time. The fire has burnt out, leaving the room chilled. My book lies face down on the floor beside me, pages splayed open, forgotten. It takes me several moments to recall where I am. I only remember the feeling of Akin's eyes locked on mine, the pressure of his pain pressing into my chest.

My breath comes in short, uneven bursts. My body is slick with sweat. My hands tremble as I push them into my hair, pressing my fingertips against my scalp like I can force the vision out of my mind. But it wasn't a vision. Not really.

It wasn't anything like my Sight has ever shown me before. It was very disjointed and raw. If I could dream, I would probably say it was a nightmare.

I lean forward, elbows braced on my knees, and press my fingers to my temples. The headache is already blooming behind my eyes. I blink against the weight of it and try to steady my breathing.

It couldn't have been real. It doesn't make sense. But the memory of it is so vivid and sharp. It felt real. It felt like he was right there in front of me.

Help me.

The words won't leave my head.

I squeeze my eyes shut and try to rationalize it. Maybe it was just my guilt, still lingering. I've spent every waking moment since his death wishing I'd seen it coming, that I'd been able to stop it from happening. I've driven myself mad wishing my Sight hadn't failed me when it mattered most. Maybe my grief has finally warped my mind enough to manufacture illusions, or hallucinations.

But even as I tell myself that, I know it's not the truth. This wasn't a fantasy or a delusion, not a dream or a nightmare. It was a message. Maybe not from the Sight, maybe from Akin's soul directly to mine. Somewhere out there, he's still alive and he's fighting to stay that way.

He's also trapped. Those shadows, those wisps of smoke, are keeping him chained in some kind of prison. It may be physical, or it may be mental. There's truly no way of knowing for sure. Either way, he is a prisoner and he needs help. He needs help from me.

I rise from the chair, my limbs aching with fatigue. My legs are unsteady beneath me, but I move anyway, dragging myself across the silent floor to the map on the far wall. It's an ancient diagram of the kingdoms, sketched in runes older than our borders. My eyes scan the outlines of Altinna and Oceana, of the neutral lands between, and then drift beyond them, to the unmarked places.

This is a dark, ancient magic. It's a shadow magic like what Eirliwyn possesses. Perhaps it's him who keeps Akin trapped. I must find him, and I must save Akin.

LIGHT IN THE DARKNESS

The walls are closing in around me. I feel it even when I stand outside on the balcony, when the sky yawns wide above me and the wind tugs at my hair. It is not the stone and mortar that smother me. It is something deeper. Heavier. It settles in my chest like a second heart, pulsing with every breath I take, weighing me down until I can barely lift my head.

I cannot sleep. I cannot eat. I sit at council meetings where the generals hammer out plans and contingencies and fallback points, and I hear none of it. Their voices buzz around me like insects, persistent but meaningless. I nod when I am supposed to. I sign what they put in front of me. But none of it touches me. None of it feels real.

The barrier is failing. I can feel it splintering at the edges. It is like trying to hold back the tide with my bare hands. No matter how hard I push, the water leaks through, rising, creeping closer.

And I no longer have Akin beside me to assure me everything will be okay.

The thought carves through me with the same precision it did the moment I watched the shadows swallow him whole. No matter how many days pass, no matter how many victories we scrape from the jaws of defeat, his absence is a blade pressed against my ribs, a wound that refuses to close.

The war drags on, endless and impossible. It isn't the war outside that's weighing so heavily on me. It's the one inside of my head. I am drowning in it.

Even my family cannot reach me. They try. They sit beside me during meals I do not touch. They press their hands over mine in silent comfort. They speak in low, careful tones, like I'm made of glass and might shatter at the slightest tremor. I wish they would stop. I wish they would leave me to crack and break without witnesses.

But they won't.

I learn to endure the kindness as I endure the grief. Numbly and wordlessly, counting the moments until I can be alone again, where at least my suffering does not have to wear a mask.

It is in the quiet moments, when the castle falls into uneasy slumber, that the whispers begin.

At first, I think it's just exhaustion, a trick of the mind brought on by sleep deprivation. I have not truly rested since the night Akin fell, so plagued by nightmares and grief that I never wanted to close my eyes again. Perhaps my mind is slipping, fraying at the edges like a tapestry pulled too tight. I tell myself it is nothing. I tell myself I am stronger than this.

But the whispers do not stop. They find me in the corridors, curling up from the shadows like smoke. They follow me into my chambers, coiling around my ankles, my throat. They seep into my dreams, twisting the few moments of peace I might have found into a waking nightmare.

"You were never meant to rule."

The first time I hear it, I freeze mid step, one hand pressed against the cold stone of the hallway. I glance over my shoulder, half expecting to find someone standing there. But the corridor is empty. My pulse hammers against my throat. I shake my head and move faster.

Later, as I sit staring blindly at the reports spread across my desk, the whisper comes again.

"You are weak."

It slips beneath my skin, into my blood, lodging itself in the soft spaces where doubt already lives. I press my hands to my ears, but it does no good. The words are not spoken aloud. They are inside of me, woven into the very fabric of my thoughts.

In the nights that follow, the whispers grow louder. They become even harsher and crueler, as unrelenting as the attacks happening on our borders.

"You will fail them all."

"Your kingdom will burn because of you."

"Your remaining Three will abandon you."

I squeeze my eyes shut. I dig my nails into my palms. I whisper prayers to gods I do not believe in. None of it helps. The voices are relentless. They know every fear I have ever harbored, every secret shame I have never spoken aloud. They know about the part of me that has always doubted I was strong enough to rule. They know about the voice inside me that whispered even as a child that my mother's love was conditional, that my father's pride was fragile, that my birthright was a burden too heavy for my shoulders.

I tell myself that it is grief. That it is exhaustion. That it is nothing more than the crumbling of a mind stretched too far and too fast.

But deep down, I know better. This is not just doubt. This is not just fear.

I am coming undone by my grief. With Akin gone, I have nothing left in me to fight, and even my mind has given up on me. Whatever defenses I used to have to keep my insecurities at bay have crumbled. Akin was always there to say kind words to counteract them, to make me feel brave and strong. His death is confirmation that I am neither.

I press my hands against my skull, fingers digging into my hair, willing the voices to stop. I wish I could tear them out by the roots, excise them like a rot that has taken hold of my soul. But they do not stop. They do not even waver. They feed on my fear. They grow louder every time I falter.

They are echoes of my own voice, sharpened into knives. They are the doubts I tried to bury when I was a child, the fears I swallowed when I first realized the weight of the crown that would one day sit upon my head.

They sound like me. They are me. My own brain is so fractured it's trying to kill me.

And I do not know how to fight something that wears my face.

I sit by the window late into the night, watching the fires burn beyond the barrier, the orange glow staining the sky. The castle is silent around me, save for the occasional distant clatter of armor or the muffled sob of someone who has lost too much.

The whispers swirl around me, wrapping themselves in the folds of my cloak, burrowing into the strands of my hair.

"You will lose them all."

"You are already alone."

"You will never be enough."

I press my forehead to the cold glass and squeeze my eyes shut. I can feel my sanity slipping through my fingers like sand. I cannot hold onto it anymore. I can't hold onto anything. Not hope or strength or even the people I love.

They are trying so hard. I know they are, even if I'm not always lucid enough to acknowledge. Brook and River and Permiton all stop in to check on me throughout the day. My mother and father try to comfort me. My siblings try to make me laugh, to remind me of who I used to be. They reach for me every day. They speak my name like it still belongs to me.

But I am slipping further away with every breath. I don't know how to call myself back. I don't know if I even want to.

Maybe the whispers are right. Maybe I was never meant to bear this weight. Maybe all I have done, all I have fought for, was always going to end in ashes. Maybe Akin died for nothing. Maybe Altinna will fall because I was too weak to save it.

I curl in on myself, drawing my knees to my chest, wrapping my arms around my body like I can hold myself together by sheer force of will.

The darkness presses in. The voices grow sharper. For the first time since this war began, I am truly, deeply afraid. Not of the enemy beyond the walls, or of death, but of myself.

I sit curled in the window seat, arms wrapped around my knees, forehead pressed against the cold stone. The fire has long since burned low behind me, casting the chamber into deep, trembling shadows. The walls seem closer tonight. Pressing inward. Breathing with every panicked beat of my heart. I do not know how much longer I can endure this.

"You were never meant to rule."

"You will lose them all."

"You are weak."

"You are powerless."

"No one has ever really loved you."

"You are worthless."

I press my hands over my ears, squeezing my eyes shut, but it does nothing. They live inside me now, woven into every breath, every heartbeat. Sleep has abandoned me. Food tastes like ash.

I want it to end. I want it to end so badly that for a terrifying moment, I almost reach for the dagger tucked beneath the folds of my dress I keep for protection.

In the end, I do not lift it. I don't even have the strength to kill myself.

Instead, I curl tighter into myself, breathing ragged, waiting for the walls to finally collapse and crush me where I sit. The darkness surges, then everything goes black.

The darkness in the room deepens, blurs. My limbs feel heavy. The whispers stretch and thin until they are no longer words but pressure, a pulsing in my temples like the beat of some ancient, cruel drum.

And then I fall. Or maybe I sleep. Maybe I collapse. I don't know. All I know is that suddenly the room is gone. When I open my eyes, the world has changed.

The ground beneath me is scorched and broken. The sky above is a swirling mass of ash and flame, pulsing orange and gray. The air is thick with smoke and blood, and every breath burns. Around me, the landscape stretches into ruin. It's Altinna, but not the Altinna I've spent my life in. It's not the Altinna I love. It's a warped reflection, a battlefield riddled with the dead.

For a sickening moment, I wonder if this is a vision of the future. Is that what Altinna becomes because of me? I rise slowly, every joint aching as if I've been asleep for a hundred years. My feet crunch over shattered bone and rusted steel. A broken banner flutters weakly from a jagged post. The scent of decay hangs thick in the air.

There is no barrier here. No shimmer of protection. No hum of magic. Only silence. Only ruin.

Panic swells in my chest. So it is a vision. This is what happens to my kingdom because I'm too incompetent to rule.

"Hello?" I call out, my voice too thin in the heavy air. "Is anyone there?"

No one answers.

This has to be a dream. Or madness. Maybe the voices have finally pushed me over the edge. Maybe I've made up a whole world to escape into. Part of me wants to believe that.

But everything feels too real. The dirt smears across my hands when I touch the ground. The wind lashes through my hair. I can hear the distant echoes of battle, of steel striking steel, the cries of the wounded, the terrible silence that follows.

Then I see a lone figure, far off at first, emerging through the haze like a vision. She moves with purpose, cutting through the battlefield on a great black horse. As she approaches, the chaos seems to still around her.

She rides toward me, regal and composed, and the closer she gets, the more surreal she becomes.

She is breathtaking, with silver hair braided down her back, gleaming in the dull light. A simple crown rests atop her brow, not grand or ostentatious, but carved with ancient markings that shimmer faintly. Her eyes are silver too, like mine. For a moment, I wonder if she is an older version of me, but her eyes are also not like mine. They are ancient and wise, and kind in a way I don't think I am.

She reins in the horse just before me. For a long moment, she simply looks at me. Then she smiles.

"I have been waiting for you, Maerilee," she says.

Her voice is like velvet and thunder, soft and resounding, vibrating through the very air around us. I feel it in my bones. I can't speak. My throat closes. My body refuses to move.

She extends a hand down to me, palm open and waiting.

I should be terrified. I should run. This is madness. A hallucination. A vision conjured by grief and sleeplessness. None of this is real. But I reach for her hand anyway.

The moment our fingers touch, something shifts in me. A warmth. A knowing. It does not quiet the fear or erase the grief, but it stills me.

She pulls me effortlessly onto the horse behind her, and together, we ride into the smoke.

ALTINNA OF OLD

The horse moves swiftly beneath us, its hooves thudding against the scorched ground, but I hardly feel it. My body is solid, grounded, but the rest of me feels like smoke. The battlefield stretches endlessly in every direction, but I can't tear my eyes away from the woman seated in front of me. Her silver braid glimmers even in the dim, ashen light, and every part of her radiates calm and command.

I have never met her before. I am certain of that. And yet, something deep inside me stirs. Her presence tugs at something old, something buried in the marrow of my bones. It is not comfort exactly, but a strange sense of being known. As if she has walked beside me through every hardship, even though I know that cannot be true.

My voice is quiet when I speak. "What's your name?"

She glances over her shoulder, and when her silver eyes meet mine, it is like the world stills.

"I am Seraphira," she says simply. "Queen of the Faeblood. First daughter of the kingdom you now call Altinna."

My breath catches and I nearly fall from the horse. Seraphira. The woman who built the barrier. The ancient queen who had Four, just like me.

She turns forward again, guiding the horse around a crumbled statue whose face has long been worn away. My heart pounds in my chest. This cannot be real. This must be some fever dream spun from exhaustion and desperation.

"You're not really here," I whisper. "You can't be."

She doesn't answer me.

We ride past the fallen remains of a great wall, its stones darkened by fire. Beyond it lies a field littered with fae bodies, men and women in armor, their weapons shattered, their limbs twisted in final, desperate postures. I suck in a breath, my throat tightening.

"Where are we?" I ask. "When are we?"

She slows the horse as we move between the bodies, her expression unreadable.

"A memory," she says at last. "This war happened long before your time, but its echoes have never stopped ringing."

I can't stop staring. Some of the fallen look like soldiers I know. Their armor is older, yes, but the insignias are familiar. The magic clinging to them is Altinnian. My kingdom. My people.

"What happened?" I ask. My voice breaks on the words.

She sighs softly, the sound thick with age and pain.

"What always happens. The timeless rot of greed. We had what they wanted. Magic. Land. Power. Wealth. They came to take it. I tried to make peace, but they would not hear me. And so, we bled."

Her words ring in my ears as I look around us. I can't take it in. I don't want to. The scent of death hangs heavy in the air, and my heart aches with the weight of what I see.

"How did you stop them?" I ask.

She doesn't answer right away. We ride in silence, passing through another field of broken banners and scorched trees.

Finally, she says, "I gave everything I had. And then I gave more."

We reach the edge of a ridge, and she halts the horse there. Below us lies the heart of the battlefield, an ancient ruin now, full of ash and bones. She sits tall and still, her gaze fixed on the horizon.

"You don't believe this is real," she says quietly.

I flinch, because it's true. "I think I'm dreaming," I admit. "Or losing my mind."

She turns her head slightly, just enough for me to see the curve of her smile.

"Perhaps you are. But even dreams can carry truth."

My hands tighten around her waist. "If you're real," I say, my voice trembling, "then why now? Why me?"

She looks forward again. "Because the darkness has returned. And because you are me, Maerilee. Not in name, but in heart. In power. You were born to finish what I began."

A wave of nausea rises in me. I want to argue, to tell her that I'm not ready. That I'm not strong enough. That I can't even tell if I'm awake right now. But my mouth stays closed. My heart knows the truth, even if my mind cannot accept it.

"We don't have much time," Seraphira says. Her voice has changed. It is firmer now, more urgent. "They are watching. Listening. This moment will not last."

I start to panic. I want to ask her a thousand things. I want to stay longer. I want to understand how she did it, how she survived, how she built the barrier, how she stood so tall when everything burned.

She turns to me, her expression suddenly fierce. "I have one thing to give you," she says, "and you must not forget it."

I nod, not trusting myself to speak.

"Don't let the darkness consume you."

The words hit me like a jolt. And then everything goes still. The air freezes. The wind dies. The smoke evaporates. And I wake up.

My body jerks upright, my breath caught in my throat.

I am on the cold stone floor of my chamber, one arm half-curled beneath me, my skin damp with sweat. The fire has not moved. The coals are still low, barely glowing. I glance toward the window and see the moon, unmoved, still cradled in the same sliver of sky it held when I last looked.

I have only been asleep for a minute. Maybe less.

It makes no sense. The dream felt like hours, days even.

I press a hand to my chest, trying to steady my breathing. My heart will not stop racing.

Seraphira.

Her name sits on my tongue like a secret. Was that real? Or was it just another symptom of my madness?

I feel no different. I have no answers or solutions. All I saw was a remnant of the past, a horrific reminder of what's at stake if I don't find a way to re-erect the barrier. All of my people will die on the battlefield if I can't do this.

But then that final phrase echoes in my mind. *Don't let the darkness consume you.* I whisper it aloud to the empty room, testing the words. They aren't like the whispers. Even in my own voice, they feel foreign. It's not something I would have come up with on my own.

And for the first time in what feels like weeks, the whispers do not answer back. I crawl back into bed, feeling at peace for the first time in days. But no sooner than I close my eyes, a sharp, cruel voice whispers.

"Akin died because of you."

I jolt upright in my bed, heart slamming against my ribs, eyes wide and searching the dark. But no one is there... only the hush of my chambers and the dull whisper of the fire in the hearth. I press my hand to my chest, trying to steady my breath, but the words echo through me like a curse.

I shake my head. I tell myself it was just a dream. Just the leftover venom of a mind too exhausted to rest. But then I hear it again.

"You could have saved him."

I grab the nearest pillow and pull it over my ears, curling onto my side as though I can press the words out of my head, silence them with feathers and cotton. I whisper to myself, nonsense words, lullabies from childhood, anything to drown it out.

But sleep does not come. It doesn't matter how exhausted I am. The second I'm about to drift off, the whispers start up again.

When I do finally close my eyes, it is not rest that greets me, but flickers of silver eyes and scorched battlefields. I want to believe

Seraphira's vision was real, but right now, the darkness feels far more tangible than hope.

By the time the sun rises, I feel brittle. I drag myself from bed, my limbs slow and leaden. I barely recognize myself in the mirror. My skin is much paler than normal. My eyes are ringed with shadows, my hair limp around my shoulders. I don't try to fix it. There is no point.

The corridors are alive with noise as I walk them, a nice distraction from the relentless whispers in my head. Servants are rushing around with food baskets. Altinnian residents are talking amongst themselves, making plans for the day, trying to find some normalcy is this very abnormal situation.

"She is the reason we are losing," someone sneers.

I freeze mid-step. The voice was close. A whisper, but not in my mind. I turn toward the hallway to my left and see two guards standing near a window, speaking quietly. I walk toward them, my heartbeat sharp in my ears.

"Excuse me," I say.

They both snap to attention.

"Did one of you just say something?"

They glance at each other, then back at me, brows drawn.

"No, Your Highness," one replies. "Not to you."

The other shakes his head.

"We were just talking about the rations, Princess."

I nod slowly, though it doesn't feel true. I continue walking.

In the great hall, I pass a pair of nobles from the outer provinces, and one of them says, "Her mother should have passed the crown to Jimmen."

I spin around, my voice sharper than I intend. "What did you say?"

The man startles. His companion takes a step back.

"I said nothing, Your Highness," he stammers. "Only that the stew last night lacked salt. But we are so grateful for your kindness, we really don't mean to complain!"

But I know what I heard. The voices are no longer whispers in my head. They follow me everywhere now. Hissing at the edges of my consciousness. Sliding into conversations like vipers. I try to tell myself it is just my mind unraveling. That the grief and lack of sleep have finally broken something inside me. But it is harder to believe that when I see lips moving. Faces turning. And then nothing.

"You will never be enough."

I hear it behind me as I sit in council.

"Akin died for nothing."

I hear it in the training yard as I pass a group of soldiers.

"Your mother should have chosen Carmelina."

It wraps around me like a second skin. I cannot breathe without hearing it. I cannot move without flinching, wondering who will be next to speak the words that stab straight into my chest.

I try to pretend. I sit at my desk and stare at maps. I sign documents with a shaking hand. I nod through strategy briefings without hearing a word. I keep my face composed because if I let it crack even once, I am afraid I will fall apart completely.

But the words keep coming, and they are growing louder.

By late afternoon, I find myself alone in my chambers, staring at nothing, fingers curled around the edge of my desk so tightly my knuckles ache. My nails dig into the wood. I do not let go. The whispers ring through the room like bells.

"She is breaking."

"She was never fit to rule."

"Akin's blood is on her hands."

I press my palms to my temples and squeeze my eyes shut. I rock forward in the chair, my breath shallow, my whole body trembling. It isn't real. It cannot be real. I am just tired. Just worn down to the marrow. This is what happens when queens do not rest.

"You're unraveling," I whisper to myself. "You just need sleep."

But I know it's more than that. It's worse than that. Something is wrong with me.

And then I see him. In the far corner of the room, half in shadow, leaning casually against the wall is Eirliwyn. He looks as he always has. He's trim, elegant, and composed as always. He wears robes as dark as night and his expression is unreadable. But there is something more sinister about him.

The Eirliwyn I knew, before he tried to kill my mother, of course, always had a sharp look on his face. He was slow to speak, but quick to discipline. He never liked me much, and made it clear to my mother that he thought I was too young and inexperienced to start training to take over Altinna. He always resented me, and after he poisoned Mother, I realized it was because I was the daughter of the man she chose over him.

Now, there's only unbridled disdain in his expression. He's dripping with it. And beneath that, is glee. He relishes in my misery.

"You look tired, Your Highness," he says smoothly. "You should rest."

I stand, the chair scraping loudly across the stone. Eirliwyn isn't here, he can't be. Last we saw him, he'd disappeared in a haze of shadows. We've been told that he's working for our enemies, but he can't have gotten into the castle without detection. He's a figment of my insanity, nothing more.

"Get out," I scream. "You're not real."

He doesn't move. I pick up something to throw at him, but it just hits the wall and shatters. I rub my eyes, and he's gone. The corner where he stood is empty. The shadows are just shadows.

The breath tears from my lungs. My knees give out and I sink to the floor, sobbing into my hands. Great, shaking gasps that tear at my throat and shake my shoulders.

I'm losing my mind, and no one can save me.

HOLD ON

River

Something is wrong with Maerilee.

I've seen grief before. I've watched fae crumple under the weight of it, drown in it, try to fight through it. I've seen it wear them down until they're hollow-eyed and brittle-boned, until they become someone else entirely.

I knew when Akin fell that Maerilee would need time, that even someone as strong as her couldn't be expected to carry on like nothing happened. But this isn't grief. This is something much worse.

I watch her from the edge of the courtyard, where she stands with her back to the firelight, her arms folded tight against her ribs like she's trying to keep herself from shaking apart. She speaks to no one, barely moves, just stares out into the darkness beyond the castle walls like she's waiting for it to come to life and swallow her whole.

Even when she thinks no one is watching, her shoulders stay stiff, like she's constantly braced for impact. Her eyes dart to empty corners. Her lips sometimes move like she's responding to a voice only she can hear. And every time, she pales just a little more.

At first, I thought she was experiencing waking nightmares. Of course she's not sleeping. Of course, her mind would fracture a little under the weight of Akin's death. We're surrounded by enemies. The Queen has no magic. The people are scared, and the barrier is barely holding.

This morning, I saw her flinch when a servant passed by. She looked at the poor girl like she'd whispered something venomous into her ear, but the girl hadn't said a word. She kept walking, eyes downcast. And Maerilee had stood frozen for a long moment, her lips pressed tight together, her whole frame trembling like a thread pulled too tight.

She didn't speak to anyone else for the rest of the day. Not Brook or Permiton or even her parents. Certainly not me.

And while I know we're all still fighting our own individual grief, I know Brook sees it too. Even though he hadn't talked to me about it, I can tell. He watches her more closely than usual, his expression quiet and tight, his gaze flicking to her every time she moves like he's expecting her to fall. Permiton, too, looks constantly unsettled. I know a lot of it is because of his lack of vision. He can't see into her future, so he can't help her. He can't help any of us, and it makes him feel useless. But his concern still seems focused on Maerilee.

None of us have said it out loud, but we're all thinking the same thing. If Maerilee falls, Altinna falls with her. With Queen Kimalissa's power gone now, Maerilee is basically the crown. Even though the Queen hasn't officially stepped down, Maerilee is the only one who can save the kingdom. She's the one the people still believe in, even when they're losing faith in everything else.

But she's fading, and she's lost all faith in herself. It's killing me to watch.

I'm so worried about her, I can't sleep. Tonight, I pace the hall outside her chambers, restless and wired with energy I don't know what to do with. The guards nod as I pass. No one stops me anymore. I've been walking this stretch of corridor so much, I could do it with my eyes closed.

The moonlight pours through the stained-glass windows, painting the floor in patterns of blue and silver. I think about the people packed into the castle halls, sleeping shoulder to shoulder, trying to pretend their world isn't ending. I think about the Oceanan soldiers surrounding us, waiting for the barrier to fall. I think about Maerilee, the weight she carries, and the way that weight seems to be dragging her beneath the surface more and more each day.

When I round the corner again, I freeze. The door to her chambers is cracked open, and I can hear voices. Two of them, it seems. One of them is Queen Kimalissa. The other is Maerilee, but her voice is so faint I almost don't recognize it.

I approach slowly, the sound pulling me closer, and stop just outside the door. I know I shouldn't listen, that I should walk away and give them privacy, but I can't. I can't walk away from her.

Inside, the fire is low. The shadows are long and soft, and Maerilee is lying in her bed, her face turned to the side, her hands limp on top of the blanket. Kimalissa sits beside her, her elegant frame bent forward, her fingers wrapped tightly around Maerilee's hand. She looks scared.

I don't think I've ever seen the Queen look scared before.

"You can rest, Maerilee," Kimalissa whispers, her voice gentle. "You don't have to carry all of this alone. Just for a little while, let yourself rest."

Maerilee doesn't move. Her breath hitches in her chest, but she doesn't cry. Her face is pale, too still. Her lips tremble as she speaks.

"He finds me in my sleep too," she whispers back.

Kimalissa squeezes Maerilee's hand gently, but Maerilee doesn't squeeze back. She just lies there, eyes wide and unfocused, her body so still it's like she's forgotten how to move.

I think she means Akin. My chest tightens at her words. Grief is cruel like that. It slips past walls, burrows under the skin, comes for you when you're weakest, pretending to be comfort until it twists the blade all over again. Maerilee loved him more than anyone. It was always clear to us that he was her first choice. We're all bound to her, but he would've been her choice if she could have chosen.

I press my hand to the wall just outside her room, staring through the cracked door. The Queen's voice is a whisper, soft and full of fear she's trying not to show.

"You're safe now, Maerilee. I'm here. We all are."

Her voice trembles at the end, and Maerilee doesn't respond. She just stares at the wall, her eyes wide and full of fear. I can't take it anymore. I raise my hand and knock gently against the doorframe. The Queen looks up quickly. Her spine straightens, her face smoothing into a more composed mask, but I can still see the truth behind her eyes.

She's terrified for her daughter. And, somewhere deeper, she's terrified for the kingdom. She's already lost her own magic. What will it mean for the kingdom if Maerilee can't come back from this?

"May I sit with her for a while?" I ask softly.

She looks at Maerilee again, then back to me.

Without a word, she rises, brushing a strand of hair from Maerilee's face and pressing a kiss to her forehead.

"I'll be nearby," she murmurs. "Call if she needs anything."

I nod. She passes me on the way out, her steps graceful even in grief, and I slip inside, closing the door behind me. Maerilee lies on the bed, the blankets around her only half-pulled up, her hands resting on her stomach like she isn't quite sure what they're supposed to be doing.

I move closer to her, but she doesn't acknowledge me. It's like she hasn't even realized that I'm there. Does she know her mother is gone? Does she know that it's night? She's so far gone, I have to wonder if she's aware of anything happening around her.

"Maerilee?" I ask gently.

Nothing. I sit at the edge of the bed, leaning forward, trying to catch her gaze. Her eyes flick toward me, then past me, locking on the far corner of the room. Her whole body tenses when she does, like she sees something horrible there.

I whip my head around to glance in that direction, but I see nothing. Whatever she sees has her terrified, and she doesn't have the physical strength to fend it off.

"When was the last time you ate?" I ask.

No response.

"Or slept? Maerilee, you look exhausted. You need to really sleep."

Still nothing.

I exhale slowly, watching her face. Her lips twitch like she might say something, but then they press together, and her breathing stutters. My gaze flicks to the corner again, and I shift slightly so I'm closer to her line of sight.

"Who's there?" I ask, trying to keep my voice steady. "What are you seeing?"

She swallows hard.

"Eirliwyn," she whispers.

My blood chills. I turn sharply to the corner again, half-expecting to see him standing there with that smug little smile of his. But it's empty, just the stone wall and the faint glow of candlelight.

There's no one there, but she believes there is.

She looks haunted. I reach for her hand slowly, letting her see me do it, giving her every opportunity to pull away, but she doesn't. Her fingers are so very cold. Her skin feels like parchment stretched thin over bone. She's wasting away to nothing, whether because of fear or exhaustion. I don't know if I can fix her, but I want to make this better for her in any way I can.

"You don't have to worry," I tell her quietly, like I'm speaking to a frightened animal that might bolt if I raise my voice. "Whatever's going on, whatever you're seeing, I'll protect you. I swear it."

A single tear slides down her cheek, but her eyes never leave the corner. I shift closer on the bed, sliding my arm around her shoulders and pulling her gently against my chest. She resists at first, just for a second, the barest tension, but then she collapses into me like the strength has finally given out of her bones.

Her head rests just below my chin. I can feel the tremble in her breath. She's still terrified, even in the safety of my arms."

"I've got you," I murmur. "You're not alone."

She doesn't speak again, but her fingers curl slightly into the fabric of my tunic, so I hold her against me. I don't move. I don't speak. I just let her rest against me, hoping that even if she can't find her way back to herself yet, she can at least feel safe here. With me.

Minutes pass, and her breathing finally starts to even out. Her exhaustion finally wins out and her body relaxes in my arms. She falls asleep against me, and I finally feel like I can breathe.

I lean back against the headboard, keeping my arms around her, staring at the corner she couldn't stop looking at. I still don't see anything, but I believe that something is there. She believes something is there, and that's enough for me. So, I stay awake.

I watch that corner like the entire Oceanan army might come out of it, because that's what Maerilee needs right now. She needs to be believed. Something or someone is trying to steal her sanity from her, but I know she's not insane. She's grieving and raw. Her heart is broken. What happened to Akin could break anyone.

If all I can do for her is provide this brief moment of reprieve, I will. I'll keep showing up to protect her, to be strong when she can't. It's the purpose I've been searching for since this war started.

SHARED POWER

Brook

I've never been particularly close to River, to no one's surprise. He was born to be the King of Oceana, the favored child of the realm. I was born to be his spare. And that's how we existed for our entire lives before we met Maerilee.

He was always so loud and arrogant before, quick to dismiss people who don't meet his impossibly high expectations. He walked like the world was supposed to part for him, and for a long time, it did.

He's changed in these last few weeks since the war started. Hell, he changed a lot the moment he chose Maerilee over our kingdom. At first, it was hard to reconcile the fact that we would spend the rest of our lives locked into a competition for Maerilee's love. Now, though, it's clear that Maerilee's happiness is more important than any petty squabble we've had over the years. It's our duty to protect her.

And we aren't alone on this quest. We have Permiton to help us as well. While he's an enigma at best and very odd at worst, I've never disliked him. He was much colder when we met, very calculated and so wrapped up in the future that he often seemed distant in the present. But now that Maerilee is slipping through our fingers, I know that he's going to step up and help. He loves her as much as I do.

I meet them in one of the old council chambers. The walls are cracked, faded by time and war, the furniture rearranged hastily to make room for maps and reports no one has had time to fully digest. It smells like parchment and desperation.

River is already there, pacing like a caged wolf, his jaw tight and shoulders rigid. He doesn't even look up when I enter. Permiton follows just behind me, his expression unreadable, hands clasped behind his back like he's trying to hold himself together with sheer posture. We haven't spoken much since the war began, but I can see in his eyes that he, too, is not doing well.

River turns to face us, his face tense and pale.

"She's unraveling," he says with no preamble or hesitation.

I nod once, slow and quiet, because I know it's true. I've seen it in her eyes, the way they flick to empty spaces, the way she flinches at sounds no one else hears. I've heard her mutter under her breath, answer questions no one asked. Her voice is quieter, thinner. And yesterday, she looked at me like she didn't even recognize me for a moment.

"She barely eats," I say softly. "She's not sleeping, not really."

"I sat with her last night," River says softly, his expression nearly tearful, something I've never seen from him. "She finally passed out in my arms, and not because she was tired. Because she was terrified. She said he finds her in her sleep."

I look up sharply.

"He?"

River's jaw clenches again.

"Eirliwyn."

That name crackles through the room like dry lightning. Permiton goes so still, it's almost unnatural. Then, slowly, he steps forward and lowers himself into one of the worn chairs. He places both hands flat on the table, his fingertips twitching slightly.

"She's seeing Eirliwyn?" he asks, his voice quieter than usual.

River nods.

"She looked right past me into the corner of the room and whispered his name like he was standing there."

Permiton doesn't blink or breathe for a moment. Then, he says calmly, "She probably is."

A heavy silence follows. I feel my stomach twist.

River stops pacing.

"You think it's real?"

Permiton looks up. There's a weight in his gaze I don't like.

"My lack of vision has been such a distraction to me, I wasn't able to see it," he mutters, almost to himself. He leans forward, his voice just above a whisper. "Shadow magic."

My chest tightens.

"But Eirliwyn is gone," I say. "He fled. He hasn't been seen since he poisoned Queen Kimalissa. She issued a decree that he should be captured on sight. The guards are on high alert. No one's seen him."

Permiton shakes his head. "Shadow magic doesn't need to be near you to touch you. It's subtle. It seeps into your bones, into your thoughts. It wraps around your memories and turns them against you. It feeds on grief, on fear. He could be a hundred miles away, but if he's fixed on Maerilee, he could be using her grief against her."

"He's haunting her," River whispers, his eyes narrowed.

"Very likely," Permiton replies. "He's attacking her mind, making her hear and see things that no one else can see or hear. Maerilee isn't hallucinating. She's being targeted."

"Because she is the barrier now," River says quietly.

We all look at him.

"That's what this is about, isn't it?" he continues. "She's the only thing standing between Altinna and complete ruin. The Queen has no magic left. We're barely holding the border. If Maerilee breaks, the whole kingdom falls. Eirliwyn doesn't need to kill her to win. He just needs to shatter her from the inside."

My hand curls into a fist. "He's using Akin's death against her," I say bitterly. "Her grief and her guilt."

Permiton nods. "And every whisper, every shadow she sees, every imagined voice… is all real. It's a targeted attack, a weapon created specifically to destroy her."

"This isn't just shadow magic," I murmur. "It's part of the war."

River turns, his eyes narrowing. "What are you talking about?"

I lean both hands on the table, staring at the scattered map but not really seeing it.

"Eirliwyn isn't just attacking Maerilee because he hates her. He's trying to kill her. Not with a sword. Not in battle. But here." I tap my temple. "He's turning her mind against her. And he's doing it while the rest of Diereken's army chips away at the kingdom's defenses."

Permiton's breath catches and he curses, something I've never heard him do, his voice low and sharp as he slams his hand flat against the table.

A pulse of light bursts from his palm.

It isn't bright, more like the sparks that come when trying to rub two stones together for a fire. It wouldn't be so strange, except that he doesn't possess this kind of magic. He's strictly a seer.

The three of us freeze.

River's eyes widen. "What the hell was that?"

Permiton is staring down at his hand like it doesn't belong to him. His fingers twitch. His brow furrows. "I'm not sure," he says, mystified.

I swallow hard. "Have you ever done that before?"

"No." Permiton exhales. "I don't have physical magic. I never have."

River's voice is tight with disbelief. "You've never had trouble with your visions before, either. What if . . . no. That's not possible."

We turn to stare at him, hoping he'll finish his thought. He stares back at us in bewilderment, as if he's afraid to share his theory.

"What is it, River?" I encourage him. "What are you thinking?"

"I've seen magic like that… from Maerilee," he finally admits. "What if, somehow, you've accessed her powers?"

I blink, trying to process it. "Has this ever happened before?" I ask Permiton.

He shakes his head. "But things have been changing," he says carefully. "I haven't had visions, but I've had nightmares. And I've felt this strange surge of energy lately, but I couldn't understand where it came from. River, you might be onto something."

River lights up at this. He's not widely known for his brains. Even I have to admit that it's a good theory.

River presses a hand to the back of his neck. "Is this even possible?" he wonders aloud.

Permiton glances between us.

"I've never heard of it," he admits, though it doesn't seem to damper his hope. "But until recently, I'd never heard of a fae with four Ones. There's not much written about Queen Seraphira and her Four, so it's possible that they had a similar bond. Maybe they all had access to each other's powers."

"We don't have time to find out," River grumbles. "We're losing her more and more each day, and Eirliwyn isn't going to stop until she kills herself or the generals declare her mentally unfit. We have to do something to bring her back from the brink."

"It would be so much simpler if I could access my Sight." Permiton sighs, dropping his hands into his hands and rubbing his temples as if that might help restore his powers.

An idea pops into my head, so crazy and reckless that it feels like something River would think of. But desperation has bred a need for action in me, and I can't help but voice my thought.

"If you can access Maerilee's powers, what if I can access yours?" I ask Permiton.

Two pairs of eyes blink back at me like I've grown an extra head.

NEW SIGHT

Brook

"What if I can tap into your Sight?"

River groans as if I've said the stupidest thing he's ever heard. I've heard that groan a lot in my life, but I've also been right more than I've been wrong.

"It doesn't work that way," Permiton says carefully, as though he's afraid I'll break if he pushes too hard. "The Sight is innate. I was born with it. It's not some reservoir you can just dip into."

"Maerilee was born with her own magic," I point out. "That didn't stop you from pulling on it. Not everything is as black and white as you make it seem."

Permiton opens his mouth to argue, but he quickly shuts it as he seems to realize he has no retort. I press forward, feeling more confident about my idea. I can't say what it is, exactly, but there's a hope brewing in me that I haven't felt in ages.

"You weren't born with the power to manipulate force. You still used hers. It was faint, sure, but it was definitely not a power that you've ever had before. If you can reach across the bond and tap into something foreign to you, why can't I?"

I don't know what I'm expecting to happen. I'm not trained in anything like this. My magic is and always has been water. It's fluid, malleable, able to shape and form into any weapon I need at the time. But water magic can't save Maerilee right now, and Sight could. If Permiton can't access it, what danger is there in me trying?

"You'll have to clear your head," Permiton finally says. "If there are any thoughts to distract you from seeing the future, you won't be able to focus on what you need to see."

I nod and take a breath, sinking into one of the heavy chairs and closing my eyes. As difficult as it is, I force every thought out of my head until there's nothing there.

"Breathe deeply," Permiton says gently, his voice low, calming. "Don't chase the Sight. Let it come to you. It doesn't answer to force. It opens to intention."

I let his words anchor me. Nothing happens at first, and I try not to feel ridiculous. If this doesn't work, we aren't any worse off than we were before. But if it could work, we could save Maerilee.

I take another deep breath, imagining myself sitting in the middle of my empty mind, waiting for the Sight to open to me. Sound disappears, color fades. Only darkness remains. And then, a light shines somewhere in the recesses of my brain.

I heed Permiton's word. I don't chase after it. I let it wash over me, until I'm no longer in my own mind, but somewhere else I've never seen in my life.

Shadows coil around me like smoke. They move as if they're alive, tasting the air, shifting just out of reach. They're not dangerous to me, but I feel their impending doom in my gut. There's a sentience behind them. A hunger.

Then the mist thickens.

Shapes form.

I see a figure emerge from the dark, and at first, I can't place him. He's slumped over, one arm twisted unnaturally behind his back, but his shoulders are broad and powerful. His face is bloodied and bruised, but unmistakable. My heart stops.

It's Akin.

Is this the future? How could it be? He's dead. Or is he? Maybe it was just another trick by Eirliwyn.

I walk closer to him. His body is rigid, locked in place by coils of shadow that move like they're breathing. They slither around his limbs and his throat and his chest, holding him in place. His eyes are open, burning with light. They're glowing alive with something fierce and terrible. As if he's fighting whatever great evil has him trapped.

Somewhere, through the haze of vision, I feel my fingers curl into fists. Akin is alive after all, and he's alone. The shadows fight to hold him, but he resists.

But suddenly, the light changes, and I see the three of us. Me, River, and Permiton, moving through the darkness, wading into the thick of it. We find him and save him. Whatever it takes us to get to him seems to wear on us, but the moment we find him, we fight through it and bring him home. We free him from his shadowy prison.

It feels so real and close, I reach out for him, try to say something to him, but the moment I do, it's like my body is pulled backward. In a sickening moment of dizziness, I'm back in the room, back in the present.

I gasp, my chest heaving like I've surfaced from deep underwater. I try to stand up, but I immediately stumble, knees buckling, and River is there, catching my arm before I collapse. Permiton is already rounding the table, eyes wide.

"What happened?" River demands.

I try to speak, but my voice won't work. My hands are still trembling.

"Brook," Permiton says sharply, gripping my shoulder. "What did you see?"

I blink up at them. The fear is still in my chest, but beneath it is something much stronger and more potent. Hope.

"He's alive," I whisper. "Akin's alive."

Their faces pale.

River's grip tightens on my arm. "Are you sure?"

I nod, breath still catching. "He's not dead. He's trapped somewhere by shadow magic. It has him bound. But he's still fighting. I saw him."

Permiton takes a step back, visibly shaken. "He can't fight forever."

"No," I agree, remembering how weary his body looked. "But he doesn't have to. I saw us too. We find him and we save him."

Permiton looks at me, something flickering behind his eyes. "You actually accessed the Sight," he whispers, marvel evident in his voice. "I suddenly believe anything is possible."

"I don't know about everything," I manage to say. "But I do know that Akin's still alive out there, and we're his only chance. And maybe if we can bring him back, he can save Maerilee."

River

The words hit me like a hammer to the chest.

"Akin's alive."

They ring in my ears, in my skull, echoing with enough force to knock the breath from my lungs. The blood drains from my face. My heart stutters once and then slams forward, thundering so hard in my ribcage I think it might burst.

Akin is alive, and he could be the answer to everything.

My hands move before my brain can catch up, and suddenly I'm gripping Brook by the arms, harder than I mean to. My fingers dig into his coat, into the muscle beneath, grounding myself in his presence like he's the only solid thing left in a world that's just spun off its axis.

"Are you sure?" I demand.

He doesn't even flinch.

His eyes are wide, still rimmed with the shimmer of whatever power just dragged him into that vision, but his voice is steady.

He and Permiton go back and forth for a moment, but he finally says the words we need to finally move forward. Akin can save Maerilee. We've tried. We've racked our brains to try to figure out how to reach her, but Akin can do it. He knows her better than any of us. She needs him for her own survival.

"Gods," Permiton whispers, lifting himself up from the chair with stiff hands and a look on his face I've never seen before. He looks just as haunted as Maerilee has lately. "I thought I saw him too," he says, voice barely above a whisper. "A few nights ago. I thought it was a nightmare. I couldn't make sense of it. My Sight has been fractured since the day he fell. I assumed I was just processing my grief ."

Brook turns to him, looking almost hurt. "You didn't say anything about it to us."

Permiton shakes his head. "Would you have believed me?" he asks defensively. "I didn't even believe myself."

He has a point, but it suddenly hits me how much we all hide from each other. This is the first time the three of us have been alone since the war started. We let Akin's death fracture us as much as it fractured Maerilee's psyche. But if Bright Waters taught me anything, it's that we're stronger together.

I pace a tight circle, hands curled into fists. I want to feel relief. Gods, I want it. But I can't feel it just yet. Not while he's still out there, chained in shadows, suffering who knows what kind of torment. Relief can come later. Right now, urgency is much more important. Because if he's alive, he may not have much time left.

"Where is he?" I ask, turning to Brook. "Did the vision show you where?"

Brook swallows. His shoulders tense. "No," he says. "Not clearly. It was all shadows. All I saw clearly was him and us. He was in bondage, and we fought through the shadows to find him. But the vision wasn't specific. It gave me the what, but not the where."

"Sight is often like that," Permiton murmurs. "You have to be patient with it, to seek it again and again until you have all the information you need."

"You need to try again," I say desperately. "We have to be able to find him."

He doesn't argue. He just nods, his expression tightening with determination as he moves to sit again. He closes his eyes, taking a deep breath. I watch his brow furrow, his lips part slightly, his hands settle on his thighs.

Permiton moves beside him, instructing him. "You did good before," he assures him. "Breathe again and let yourself be taken back to the place you were before. Be careful not to interact too much with what you see, or the Vision might fade."

I remain silent, standing behind them, my entire body thrumming with impatience I don't dare unleash. I want to grab a sword. I want to storm whatever hell Akin is trapped in and tear it apart with my bare hands. But I can't storm anywhere without a location. I have no choice but to be patient.

A breath passes. Then two. Brook's breathing slows. His hands twitch. And then he gasps, jerking upright like something just pierced his chest.

Permiton reaches out, steadying him. "What did you see?" he asks.

Brook shakes his head, eyes still glazed with power. "Still shadows. But I think it's near water. The air felt heavy, wet and cold."

"The Oceanan borderlands?" I ask.

"No," Brook says confidently. "It was too quiet for that. And it felt near, but somewhere hidden. But now it's like I feel this thread in my chest." He pats his chest and looks up at Permiton curiously. "Can Sight lead us physically?"

"I would believe anything at this point," he mutters. "It's never quite worked like that for me, but you have different magic inside of you. If you feel like you're being led somewhere, I suggest you follow that intuition."

"So let's go," I say. "The three of us. Now. We have no time to waste! We have no idea how much time he has left."

Permiton nods. "We'll follow the pull of the vision," he confirms with Brook.

"I'll find him," Brook says. "I swear I will."

My jaw tightens. "Great," I say impatiently, grabbing for my sword. "I'll tell Maerilee he's alive and we'll go after him."

But before I reach the door, Brook speaks again, his voice commanding. "Wait."

I turn back. His eyes meet mine.

"We can't tell her," he says gravely. "If, for some reason, we can't save him, it'll kill her. If we're going to do this, we can't say anything to her until we're sure we've succeeded."

"She'll want to come," Permiton adds. "She'll insist. But she's not ready. She's hanging on by threads. If we leave and fail—"

"She'll break," I finish softly, nodding at their wisdom.

She can't know. Not unless it's a success.

Not unless we bring him back.

"Then we don't tell her," I say.

"We bring him home," Brook replies.

Permiton sets a hand on the map. "And gods help Eirliwyn if we fail."

CREEPING INSANITY

Maerilee

The whispers never stop. Even when the room is quiet, even when the halls are empty, they slither through the cracks of my mind like vines. Cold. Coiling. Rooting deeper with every breath I take.

"You are too weak."

"You let him die."

"You will never be enough."

"You should kill yourself."

The last one hits hardest. I flinch, curling tighter into myself, my knees drawn to my chest atop the cold stone of my chamber floor. My fingernails dig into my scalp as I clutch at my temples, shaking from the force of it, the weight of it. I know the thoughts aren't mine now. I know they don't belong to me.

But they still feel true. Each word lands like a blade, sharpened by grief. My body trembles. I can feel the pressure of the darkness pressing in from all sides, on my lungs, my skin, my spine. It creeps like oil across every surface. It wants me silent, broken, hollowed out.

But somewhere deep inside of me, there's a spark, igniting me to push back. It's flickering and weak, but it burns nonetheless.

A voice, different than the others, and much stronger, commands me in the midst of the storm.

"Do not give into the darkness."

It doesn't sound like it's coming from inside me, the way the whispers do. It reverberates around the room, vibrates under the floor. It's an earthquake that shakes me from this hell I've been in for days.

My head snaps up, and I feel her before I lay eyes on her. Queen Seraphira stands in the middle of the room, regal and strong. She's as tall and regal as I remember from my dream of her. Her silver braid hangs over one shoulder, catching the glint of a light that doesn't exist in this room. Her eyes are starlight and steel, fixed on me like they already know the outcome of this battle and will not allow me to lose it.

The darkness rears around her, growing thicker, snarling as if it senses the threat of her presence. It becomes physical, shadows whipping around her in a frenzy, but never quite touching her light. The whispers become louder, harsher.

"She cannot save you."

"You are alone."

"You are nothing."

They are no longer whispers, but roars, like a strong wind bent on destroying everything in its path.

"This is not real, child," Seraphira says, and her voice is not cruel or coddling, but full of clarity. "You are stronger than this. They only win if you let them."

My throat tightens. I try to speak, but the words choke behind a dam of pain. My hands still tremble. My knees are still buckled. A part of me still believes the whispers because they sound like me. They use my voice.

"You don't know what I've lost," I whisper. "You don't know how much it hurts."

Seraphira steps forward, unfazed by the shadows curling at her feet.

"I do."

Her voice is quieter now. A thread of memory. A reminder.

"I fought this same battle once, Maerilee. I stood where you stand now. I was nearly lost to it. But I rose. And so must you."

"I can't," I say, even as my hands curl into fists.

"You can," she assures me, in a voice that isn't sound, but light. It's ancient, full of power older than the world itself. "Rise."

I stare at her, at the woman I've seen only in dreams and fragments, in stories whispered by advisors who didn't even bother to learn her name. She is the original queen. She carved peace from chaos. She created the barrier, and she found the strength within herself to keep the kingdom safe for centuries.

She is not a vision or a memory or a fragment. She is real and light, and her power is pushing back the darkness of Eirliwyn's attack. The shadows become nothing more than wisps around her. The whispers fade into silence.

But just as I'm ready to heed her command, the darkness shrieks, rushing toward me. The pressure builds until it feels like my ribs might snap, like the floor might crack beneath me. I realize, this is its last stand. If I do as Seraphira says, I will be free.

So I don't close my eyes. I plant my hands on the stone and push, not just with my arms, but with everything inside me., with every ounce of fury I've buried under sorrow, with every drop of love I still carry for my people, for my Four, and for myself.

With every memory of Akin's hands, River's eyes, Brook's smile, Permiton's voice.

I scream. Light bursts from my chest, from my fingertips, from the soles of my feet. It floods the room, slamming into the shadows like a tidal wave of fire. The whispers howl in rage as the magic tears them apart, shattering them into dust.

And then there's silence. Real, empty silence. The whispers are completely gone. The only sound I hear is my ragged breath. But Seraphira doesn't disappear. She remains in the center of my room, watching me with a soft expression.

My knees give out. I collapse back to the floor, but not in defeat. This time, I fall from exhaustion. The spell is broken, and I have survived it.

"I didn't think I could do it," I whisper, voice raw.

"You are not alone, Maerilee. You never will be."

I look up at her, heart still racing. "You're not a dream, are you?"

She kneels beside me, her presence a balm. "No."

"Then what are you?"

Seraphira smiles faintly, something ancient flickering in her expression. "I am memory. I am magic. I am your bloodline. I am everything that came before you."

I stare at her, wide-eyed. "Why now? Why me?"

"Because you are the one who will save Altinna, just as I did," she answers fiercely, her face just inches from mine.

I want to ask her more. I want to keep her here forever. But then there's a sharp knock on my bedroom door.

Seraphira fades instantly, as if the knock pushed her into mist. But the light she left behind stays. It hums beneath my skin, wrapping around my ribs, settling behind my eyes. I'm still shaking, but I'm no longer afraid.

I walk to the door with more strength than I've felt in weeks.

River

I don't expect her to answer the door when I knock. It was more of a courtesy than anything, since I've barely seen her out of bed in weeks. But the moment the door opens, I know something's changed.

She's standing there, eyes clear, cheeks flushed, hair mussed like she just woke up, but her shoulders aren't hunched. Her breathing isn't ragged. And when she sees me, she jumps into my arms.

I catch her on instinct, arms winding tightly around her back as her body presses into mine.

For a moment, I forget how to breathe.

"You—" I start to say, but I don't finish, because this is new and exciting and interesting.

For as long as we've known each other, there's been passion, sure, but never this level of intimacy. It's only the second time she's seemed genuinely happy to see me, and the first was when I almost died.

Now she's holding on like I'm the air she's been missing. She pulls back just enough to look up at me, her silver eyes brighter than I've seen them in weeks.

I stare at her, stunned. "What happened?" I can't help but ask, surging with joy at the drastic change in her demeanor.

"It's hard to explain," she answers with a smile, releasing me without any hint of awkwardness or regret. "But I'm me again. That's all I really know."

"I thought I'd lost you," I say before I can stop myself. "Maerilee, I thought I'd lost you forever."

I reach down and tuck a strand of hair behind her ear. My hand lingers on her cheek, just a little too long, but she doesn't pull away.

"I've been so damn scared," I whisper. "You kept slipping further and further, and I couldn't do anything to stop it. I didn't know if you were going to come back to me."

"I wasn't sure either," she admits, her light dimming just slightly as she remembers the darkness that so recently drowned her.

Suddenly, I can't hold it in anymore. "I love you," I say, without any insecurity or shame.

Her breath catches.

My voice is rough with emotion I can't name, let alone explain.

"I love you, Maerilee," I continue. "I don't know exactly when or how it happened, but I've come to realize that I can't live without you. I don't want to live without you. And when I almost lost you, I saw what life without you would entail, and I was ready to go out to the front lines and offer myself as a sacrifice."

Her eyes are wide, her lips slightly parted. She opens her mouth to say something, but the words don't come. They don't need to. Because in the next moment, she kisses me hard and rough, clinging to me desperately.

It's not soft or hesitant. It's raw, like something that's been burning under the surface finally igniting. Her hands tangle in my hair as I pull her closer, backing her into the room and slamming the door behind us with my foot.

She gasps when my mouth moves to her throat, her back pressing into the nearest wall. My hands find her waist, her thighs, lifting her until her legs wrap around me and her fingers dig into my shoulders like she can't bear to let go.

"I never want to be without you," I growl against her skin.

"Gods, River, I need you," she breathes out in a wisp.

She grabs at my clothes, and I hear buttons popping and fabric tearing. I couldn't care less. I would burn my entire wardrobe for her if she asked me to. In fact, I would do anything if she asked me to.

She relaxes her legs until she's standing in front of me, pulling me down with her to the bed, and the world narrows to the space between our bodies, the fire in our skin, the tension that's been building for far too long. I hover on top of her, the anticipation between us unbearable, but then she forces me back on the bed, climbing on top of my lap.

Gods, I'm rock hard already, my erection straining against my pants. She seems to notice, deftly pulling at my trousers until I'm free. She meets my eyes wickedly, then gently palms me. My head falls back lazily as I let myself get lost in the feel of her.

"Open your eyes," she commands. "No more darkness."

I look down at her and nearly explode when she pulls me into her mouth and swirls her tongue against my head.

"You don't have to do that," I rasp, though I can't imagine her stopping.

"I want to," she whispers.

"I want to feel you," I complain, tugging her back up so she's hovering over my lap again. "I want to be inside of you."

Her eyes darken as she kisses me. I can taste the saltiness of my precum on her lips. I run my fingers through her silky hair, trying to find any purchase. She reaches down to hike up her skirts and pulls them up around her waist. She positions herself on top of me, slowly inching down onto me, nearly robbing me of my breath.

And then she's moving wildly, hungrily, and our hands and mouths find places only we are meant to touch. Her breath hitches as I thrust into her, her body arching, my name falling from her lips like a curse and a prayer all at once.

I brace my hands on either side of her hips, watching her eyes flutter open, her expression raw and bare.

"I've got you," I whisper.

She nods, trembling on top of me. "Don't let go," she pleads, her hands holding onto mine tightly as she rides me like one of the royal horses.

"Never," I promise her.

We move together, not just in rhythm, but in understanding. In shared pain and healing. In all the things we were never brave enough to say until now. I lean up to kiss her hard. She clutches me harder.

And when she falls apart on top of me, her voice breaking in a sob that sounds like freedom, I follow her over the edge, burying my face in her neck and holding on like my life depends on it.

Maybe it does.

As she comes down, her breath still coming out in pants, she says, "In case I didn't say it before, I love you too."

She snakes her arms around my neck and kisses me harder than before. My heart pounds in my chest, from our exertions and her words. I tuck another strand behind her hair and watch her face carefully, unable to believe that I'm lucky enough to be loved by her.

IN THE RUINS

Permiton

Our plan is terrible. It's risky and rushed, based more on instinct than certainty. Still, it's the only one we have. I stare down at the ancient text splayed across the marble table, the brittle parchment threatening to crumble beneath my fingers. The ink has faded in places, the script so old it bleeds together like veins across stone, but I've read it four times through, and I keep coming back to the same haunting phrase.

"Shadow that clings can be burned by light unclaimed."

Light unclaimed. Not wielded. Not conjured. Unclaimed.

It's maddening and vague. One of those half-riddles the old scholars always loved to leave behind as though ambiguity made them brilliant instead of insufferable. Without my Sight, I have no way of knowing what it really means.

I stand in the ruins of what used to be a steady gift. Where once I could see clear branches of possibility, now all I get are flickers, blurred images that are dreams I forget the second I wake. I thought it was grief, at first, that my guilt over Akin's "death" was too heavy a veil for my visions to pierce.

But now I think it's something else, something darker. The

shadows that have hold of Akin aren't just cloaking him. They're interfering with me too, cloaking my Sight. The more I think about it, the more certain I am that Eirliwyn's goal wasn't to kill Akin. He wanted to do so much more. He wanted to erase him from existence.

What he didn't anticipate was that Akin would keep fighting.

Brook saw it. I felt it. Somewhere inside that vision, the half-nightmare I tried to forget, I saw him burning. His light struggled against the shadows like a star pressed beneath a tide of smoke. He isn't lost yet. And as long as he's not lost to us, we have to do anything we can to get him back. But if we wait any longer, he'll be gone forever.

I glance back down at the spell. It's ancient, probably forbidden. There are symbols along the margins that predate the Altinnian dialect, maybe even the foundation of the barrier itself. And it doesn't just require magic.

It requires faith. That's what terrifies me most. We have to have faith in ourselves. Faith in Akin.

I close the book and tuck it into the satchel hanging at my side. The edges poke into my ribs, grounding me in the moment, reminding me that we don't have time for precision. We don't have time for second-guessing.

I turn toward the door and make my way through the palace corridors, the weight of every footstep settling in my spine. The halls are quiet now, the people lulled into some strange sense of normalcy. I don't look at them as I make my way toward the front door.

When I reach the east courtyard, Brook is already there. He's pacing. His hands twitch at his sides, water rippling across his fingertips even though there's no source nearby. He's jittery, on edge, but focused.

River is slower to arrive. He doesn't say much when he steps into the clearing, but his jaw is tight, and his eyes are storm-dark. He carries his sword strapped across his back, his movements sharp, efficient, and ready for war.

"Are we all ready to go?" I ask. "Hopefully you've all packed light.

We'll be crossing into no-man's land. Once we reach the far side of the eastern ridge, we'll need to move on foot."

River nods.

"And Brook, you know where you're going?"

"No," he admits. "Not exactly. But I know where the magic is thickest. It's like a feeling that's guiding me forward. Permiton, have you found anything in the texts that might help us?"

I pull the book from my satchel, careful not to let the wind catch its edges.

"It's old," I tell them. "And dangerous. It doesn't pull the shadows off. It burns them. It should free Akin, but–"

"That sounds like it could kill him," River interjects before I'm done speaking, his brows furrowed.

"It could," I say honestly. "But if we do nothing, he will die. Eirliwyn might actually succeed in ripping him from reality forever."

Brook runs a hand through his hair. "Then it's time for us to go," he says, making his way to the gates. Once we go past them, we'll officially be on our own, possibly on a suicide mission.

Silence stretches for a breath.

And then River steps forward. "What do you need from us?"

I'm surprised by his willingness to help. He's changed so much recently, and he's not fighting me on this. He doesn't question the scroll or the source or whether or not I'm stable enough to do this after everything. He just believes in me. He already has faith.

"We'll need to form a triad," I say. "I'll cast the spell. But it needs anchors. Both of you. You're both connected to Akin and to Maerilee. That's the bond the spell will pull from."

River nods. Brook doesn't hesitate either.

"Better sooner than later," River grunts, following Brook toward the gate.

I stare at them for a long moment, the weight of their trust pressing against the aching uncertainty in my chest.

We'll either save Akin or die trying.

Brook

Crossing the barrier is like stepping into another world. The moment my boot clears the magical threshold, I feel everything change. The air thickens, presses against my chest like smoke after a fire. It smells of old blood and scorched stone, of water magic twisted into something sharp and unnatural. The wind carries the faintest echo of screams, like ghosts still roaming the battlefield, waiting for someone to remember them.

My fingers tighten around the hilt of my sword.

I shouldn't be this tense. I know that our forces are miles away, fighting our enemy forces. We won't see any battle here, so that's a plus. But there's the feeling of death all around us, and I can't help but be overwhelmed by it. I try to push it aside and just focus on the pull in my chest.

Behind me, River adjusts the straps on his shoulders, checking the sheath of his blade with a precision that tells me he's feeling it too. Permiton stands just ahead, his eyes glowing faintly with borrowed magic as he raises a trembling hand.

The air warps around his fingers.

A faint and silvery shimmer extends outward like a dome, wrapping around us. It pulses against the terrain, camouflaging us from detection. It's Maerilee's magic. Or maybe it's his now too. Everything's bleeding together lately.

"It's holding steady," Permiton mutters, sweat already beading at his temple. "But it's hard to maintain. It's like the atmosphere is pushing down on it."

"Maybe it is. Maybe they've even found a way to make the terrain fight against us," River says grimly.

"We're getting closer," I cut in. "The magic is getting stronger. We're close."

We walk in silence for a long stretch, the only sounds are our footsteps crunching against cracked earth and the occasional caw of a distant crow. I keep my eyes moving, scanning the ridges, the tree line, every ruined watchtower for signs of movement. But the land is barren and dead, like something came through and drained the life out of it.

As we get closer, we spot a ruin rising up in the distance. The moment I see it, I immediately know that Akin is hidden there. It's like the magic is moving my legs without my permission. This is definitely the place.

It looks like it was once a temple or a fortress long ago, but now it's crumbled into jagged edges and half-swallowed by the earth. Ivy creeps across the broken walls, dark and bloated with whatever pollution lingers here. At the center, a great stone arch yawns open, the interior shrouded in shadow.

It looks like where I saw Akin in my vision, bound in darkness. It was hard to tell then, but now that it's in front of my eyes, I know without a doubt it's the place. The vision of Akin nearly attacks me, and I can still see him fighting, screaming, burning with light.

I slow to a stop just before the threshold. River moves to my side, jaw clenched.

"There are no guards," he says roughly. "Are we sure this is the right place?"

"I'm positive," I say, scanning the outer perimeter. "Don't be fooled. He's definitely here."

"It's too quiet," Permiton murmurs. "It shouldn't be."

He's right. This ruin should be crawling with Oceanan soldiers or Diereken's elite, anyone tasked with protecting what must be the most dangerous prisoner in their entire campaign. But there's nothing here.

"Maybe they moved him," River says, but his voice lacks conviction.

I step inside.

The shadows swallow us. The stone corridor narrows, and we move in a tighter formation, River ahead, me in the center, Permiton bringing up the rear. The silence deepens with every step. Not even rats skitter here. There are no birds, not even dripping water. There's just emptiness.

We reach the inner chamber, and it's empty.

I stop cold. The chamber is circular, with ancient runes carved into the floor, most of them corroded. The stone dais at the center is cracked down the middle, stained dark with something long dried. Shards of crystal lie scattered in the dust, and the air hums with residual magic.

But Akin isn't here.

My mouth goes dry. "This is it," I nearly scream, but I somehow manage to contain my fear.

River turns to me. "Are you sure?" he asks, not in anger, but in genuine fear.

"I saw him here," I snap, frustration rising like bile in my throat. "This was the place. I know it."

Permiton kneels beside one of the crystals, fingers brushing over its surface.

"There was shadow magic here," he confirms. "Recently. It still lingers like tar in the air."

"Has it faded?" River asks.

"It has if he's been moved," I whisper. My heart slams against my ribs. "They must have known we were coming. Maybe they have a seer on their side, too."

I imagine someone on their side watching us in their visions, waiting until we made the discovery and had real hope. And then they took him somewhere else, after we knew where he was. They let us have hope just to steal it away.

I sink to my knees beside the cracked dais, pressing my hand to the stone. It's still warm. That means we're close. Too close to give up.

"I don't understand," I mutter. "Why take him away now? Why leave the ruin undefended?"

"Because they didn't expect us to find him at all," Permiton says, rising slowly. "Because this wasn't meant to last. Holding him here was never the endgame."

River paces the chamber, running his hand through his hair. "Eirliwyn must have sensed us," he says angrily.

If there were anything for him to throw, he probably would. He looks like he might punch one of the great stone walls, but he seems to think better of it.

"Maybe they just got tired of waiting," Permiton says sadly.

I look up. "Waiting for what?"

"For us to give up," he answers gravely.

The silence that follows is deafening.

"We have to find him," I say. "There has to be something here, something left behind."

River moves toward a stone altar at the edge of the chamber. "Start looking."

We spread out around the ruin, but we come up with absolutely nothing. There are no tracks or signs anywhere that he's been taken somewhere. We go back to the dais, to mourn, to rage, to accept that he's really not here. We know we won't give up, that we can't, but for now, we can only lick our wounds.

Finally, we get up and begin our journey back to the barrier.

WHEN THE DARKNESS COMES

Akin

There is no time here. Not really. It stretches and twists and folds in on itself like smoke curling in the wind, and I've long stopped trying to measure it. I don't know how long I've been here, only that my muscles have forgotten movement and my mind has frayed at the edges more times than I can count.

Sometimes I hear my own heartbeat. Sometimes I don't. Sometimes I remember the feeling of a sword in my hand, the warmth of Maerilee's breath against my neck, the solid weight of River's shoulder brushing mine in battle. Sometimes I think they are figments of my imagination, people who never truly lived.

Here in this place, the in-between where shadow bleeds into shadow and the air pulses with silent, screaming magic, I barely exist. The darkness doesn't just cover me. It holds me. It lives in me. It wraps around my limbs like cold iron, slipping between my ribs, threading through the places I thought were mine and making them something else. My thoughts no longer come in order. My breath is ragged when I remember to take one. Even my name feels like someone else's. And always, always, are the whispers.

They used to sound like strangers. Now they sound like me.

"She's forgotten you."

"You were never the strongest."

"You were only ever her bodyguard."

I clench my teeth. Even that is a struggle. But I hold onto the thought of Maerilee. The name is an ember. It's the only thing that hasn't faded entirely. Not even when the shadows try to suck the heat from it. Not even when they press in, closer each day.

She loved me, I remember that much. I think I remember that. And gods help me, I think I loved her too.

The darkness surges suddenly, like it senses my resistance. It clamps down, a vice around my chest, and I can't breathe, can't scream, can't even think.

But then something changes. It's small, at first, just a flicker in the dark, a shiver of something different slicing through the thick black. It's a small light. A pin drop, really. But it's more than I've seen in ages. How long? Days? Weeks? Years? There's no way of knowing. Perhaps I've always existed here in this darkness.

But the light finds me. At first, I think it's a trick, another mirage crafted by the magic trying to break me. I've seen things before. I've heard Maerilee's voice when it wasn't real. I've watched dreams play across the nothing like lies projected on smoke. But this is brighter.

It doesn't whisper or mock the way the dreams did. It burns like wildfire, and with it comes footsteps.

I blink hard. Gods, even that hurts. I force my head up from where it's slumped against some unseen barrier.

The light grows, and then I see them. River, Brook, and Permiton stand out against the light, their silhouettes the best thing I've ever seen in my miserable existence. My breath punches out of me so fast, it feels like I've been stabbed.

They're here. They came for me, to find me. So, they are real. Maerilee is real. My whole life was real, which means the darkness isn't.

For a moment, the shadows recoil. They peel back like smoke meeting wind, and I feel weight slide from my shoulders, air rush into my lungs. I sit up. I move for what feels like the first time ever. My hands are mine again.

"River!" I shout, voice hoarse and ragged. "Brook! Permiton! I'm here!"

They pause in the center of the room, heads turning, searching.

Brook steps forward, his expression tight with confusion. River's blade is out. Permiton's hands glow faintly with a magic I've never seen before. They've changed in some small, imperceptible way.

"I'm here!" I yell again, stumbling toward them. "Gods, I'm right here!"

Brook tilts his head. His brow furrows. He looks almost straight at me, but he doesn't see me. They all look through me like I'm smoke, like I really don't exist.

"No," I whisper.

I step closer. I'm only a few feet away now. I reach for Brook's arm, try to grab it, but my hand passes right through it.

"No, no, no," I groan. "Dammit, no!"

They circle the room.

Permiton mutters something about residual energy. River's pacing, eyes sharp, frustrated.

Brook kneels and touches the ground, murmuring about the runes I've long stopped trying to decipher.

"I'm here!" I scream. "Please. Please, don't leave. Don't," I beg, my voice breaking.

The darkness is coming back. I feel it behind me, curling at my feet, slipping up my spine like cold hands pulling me into the floor. The warmth of their presence, of hope that I'll ever be rescued, is already fading. I scream again, but my voice breaks.

And still they don't hear me. They speak to each other in low voices. I can't make out the words. My vision blurs. My knees hit the ground. Brook shakes his head. Permiton closes his book. River looks back once more before turning.

His eyes pass over me. Right over me. And then they walk away.

I try to follow, but my legs don't work. I reach for them, but my arms won't lift. The shadows wrap around my throat, pulling me back. I scream as the last sliver of light disappears down the hall. And then I'm alone again.

I'm still here. I'm still alive, if anyone can say this is living. But I'm more lost than ever. This can't be happening. They were here. They were actually here. I saw them standing just a few feet away from me, looking for me, and they didn't know that I was right here, right in front of them.

What hell is this? I try again to move, now that I remember how. I push past the pain in my throat to scream. Maybe I can be loud enough to be heard. They can't be far.

"River!" I rasp. "Brook! Permiton! I'm right here!"

But my voice is hoarse, useless, lost in the oppressive weight of this place. The shadows clamp down again like iron, thick bands across my arms, my chest, my spine. Every breath I take is agony. The air tastes like ash, like rot, like despair.

They can't hear me. They're so close, I could reach them, if only my legs would move. But they won't. My body is still bound, half-submerged in the darkness, my magic long since strangled into silence. It's like trying to scream with a mouth full of stones.

I throw myself forward anyway.

The chains drag me back like I weigh a thousand pounds.

"No!" I shout. "Don't leave. Please don't leave!"

They return a moment later, and my hope flickers, just slightly. When they re-enter, Brook tilts his head, eyes narrowing as if he heard something faint. My breath catches. Hope flares. But then his attention shifts, flicking to the broken altar at the center of the room.

He didn't hear me.

River takes a slow lap around the room, blade drawn, brows pulled together in frustration. Permiton's eyes search around the dilapidated stones before the three of them sit down on the dais, looking defeated.

They don't see me. The darkness hums in triumph around my ankles. It knows they're going to leave, and that I'll be forgotten again.

The scream tears from my throat, raw and ragged. It doesn't matter that it hurts. It doesn't matter that my lungs burn or that my voice has been reduced to a shred of what it once was. I scream anyway.

"I'm here!" I bellow. "I'm right here, damn you!"

Nothing. Brook mutters something under his breath. Permiton responds. River glances toward the hallway.

They're about to go. Panic sets in, white-hot and blinding. I've been alone in this hell for so long. Trapped in silence. Drowning in it. I don't even know if I'm still whole. I don't know who I am anymore beyond the grief and the memory of Maerilee's hands on my face.

Her name pulses through me, the only light I've had in this cursed darkness. It sears across my skin like wildfire. And suddenly something snaps. It's not in my body, but rather in the magic that's holding me back.

Deep inside my chest, something tears open like a wound, and I feel light. It isn't the same soft, glowing warmth of healing magic I've felt before. It's brighter, more primal, like the first spark of creation. It builds fast, rising up through my lungs, my veins, my bones, demanding to be released.

I throw my head back and roar. It explodes out of me, causing the chains to scream as they break. Sound fractures the space around me, deafening and monstrous, like metal being shredded in a forge, like the cracking of the earth itself. The shadows flinch back in alarm. I see them recoil, peeling away from my wrists, my chest, my neck. I drop forward, landing hard on the stone with a jarring thud that rattles my teeth.

For the first time in weeks, maybe months, I can move. I can breathe. I brace myself on trembling arms, gasping for air, blinking against the sudden brightness. My hands shake violently, blood oozing from old wounds reopened by the strain. I feel like I'm breaking apart from the inside out.

But I'm free. And when I look up, three sets of eyes stare at me in bewilderment. River is staring straight at me, eyes wide, mouth open in stunned silence. Brook's face pales. Permiton's hand clamps around the edge of the altar like he needs to steady himself.

"That's impossible," Permiton breathes.

A single heartbeat passes. Then another. Then everything goes dark again.

The light collapses back into me with a sickening rush. My legs buckle. My lungs seize. Pain slams into me from every direction.

I collapse again, hard. The ground is cold beneath me is sticky with my blood. The last thing I see before my sight leaves completely is River rushing toward me.

I wake to the warmth of the sun, to cool water against my cracked lips. A voice murmurs something soft and frantic, something in a language I don't quite understand. My lashes flutter open slowly, the brightness stabbing into my skull like a blade.

Everything hurts. My entire being is pain. Yet, somehow, it's a stark relief compared to the nothingness I've felt for eternity.

And I'm not alone.

Permiton's face comes into focus first. He's crouched beside me, brow furrowed, an empty vial in his hand. It's his vial from Bright Waters, it has to be.

He used it on me.

"Your wounds are gone," he says, his voice low and reverent. "You might experience some residual pain, but I think you're going to be all right."

I glance down. Where there should be blood, torn flesh, and shadow-rotted gashes, there's only smooth skin. It's pale and raw, but it's still whole.

My heart stutters in my chest. It's such a joy to feel my heartbeat again, to hear it echoing in my ears.

I lift my hand and look past Permiton's shoulder. River is there, his arms crossed over his chest, his jaw clenched like he's barely holding himself together. Brook is just behind him, eyes red, but dry.

"You saw me," I rasp.

River meets my eyes, his own looking red and glassy.

"Yeah," he says, voice rough. "We saw you."

Emotion chokes me. I nod once, unable to do more. Permiton's hand settles on my shoulder.

"You broke through," he says. "You fought the shadow magic from the inside. That should have been possible."

"I don't think it would have been if I weren't so afraid of you leaving me," I tell him.

"No." Permiton sighs thoughtfully. "Something has changed in us. In all of us. We all have magic we didn't have before. It's strange."

"But not worth dwelling on right this minute," River interjects, though his voice lacks any venom. "We need to get back home. Maerilee needs you."

Maerilee. The thought of her erases all of my remaining pain. I have to get back to her, to run to her if I'm able.

The darkness kept me bound for so long, but she's the light that saved me.

STRENGTH TO CHOOSE

I'm standing back on the battlefield, smoke coiling in the air. Ash clings to my skin. The scent of blood and fire invades my lungs. My boots are caked in soot. The wind carries the soft moan of a world unraveling.

Strange. I was sure I was in my room. I must be asleep again. Sure enough, when I look across the battlefield, Seraphira is there waiting for me. She stands in the same place as before, the hem of her pale gown untouched by the carnage, her long silver braid trailing over her shoulder like a banner. Her silver eyes are piercing, unreadable, as they settle on me.

"You're back," she says, her tone making it clear that she's been expecting me.

I swallow hard. "Lately, I wish I never had to leave," I admit, knowing she'll keep my secrets. "Things out there are so awful. Every moment feels like it could be the last. The barrier is failing, and I don't know what to do about it."

She tilts her head, watching me curiously.

"Why are you so afraid, Maerilee?"

"I'm not," I answer indignantly, not appreciating her words when she has no idea what challenges we're facing in my time.

"You are," she states simply. "You doubt your own abilities, and you're afraid of failure. And I'd like to know why."

Her certainty needles under my skin, stirs something sharp in my chest. I cross my arms tightly over my body, trying to contain it, trying to keep from unraveling again.

"I'm exhausted. I've lost people I love. I'm carrying more than anyone should have to bear. That's not fear. That's reality."

"Is it?" Her voice is calm. Not mocking, just steady. "Because all I see is a girl drowning in her own power, too afraid to swim."

I snap. "I'm trying," I hiss. "You have no idea what I've done, what I've given, to protect Altinna. The man I love is dead, my mother has lost her magic, everyone is relying on me, and I am doing everything I can to survive."

"And yet you still look for someone else to save you."

The words hit harder than I expect. I stagger back a step, the echo of her voice crackling through the air like thunder. Seraphira lifts her hand. The world around us ripples, warps, reshapes into something entirely different.

The ruined battlefield bends away like melted wax, folding into itself, replaced by something else entirely. It's Altinna, but not my Altinna.

The castle stands tall, its towers gleaming white under a harsh morning sun, but the walls are scorched, blackened by flame. The air is heavy with smoke. The streets are flooded with people, warriors in golden armor clashing with shadow-cloaked enemies. Screams fill the air, sharp and distant. The city is alive and dying all at once.

Seraphira stands at the center of it all, her armor elegant and formidable, silver and flame-gold, shaped to her form perfectly. She is radiant and untouchable, the pure incarnation of power.

"This is my Altinna," she says, her voice quiet but unshakable. "Before the barrier. Before the treaties. Before peace."

I turn slowly, taking in the carnage. There's blood in the fountain where I used to play as a child. Bodies lie crumpled beside the temple steps. Soldiers rush through the streets, some shouting orders, others carrying the wounded.

"This can't be real," I whisper.

"It was," she says. "This is what I came from. This is what I stopped."

I turn to look at her, my throat thick. "How?"

Her gaze flicks behind me, and I see four figures in the distance. At first, they're only silhouettes, but they sharpen with each step, coming into the flickering light of battle. A man with dark brown skin and eyes that glow like sunlight through amber. A slender, sharp-featured man with white-blond hair and an arc of shadow dancing around his shoulders. A fae with ink-black eyes and glowing tattoos carved across his forearms. And a fourth, taller than the rest, his body cloaked in green-blue mist, water magic rolling off him in waves.

They don't speak, but they don't need to. I understand right away that they're Seraphira's Four.

They move through the chaos like gods, people seeming to part when they go by. Their bond crackles in the air. I can feel it, even from here. Each of them is connected to her and to each other, their connection unmistakable. They're a unit. They don't move as five individuals. They're a force.

Seraphira watches them with something like longing, or maybe memory. "You still think you aren't enough," she says softly. "Because you've only tasted your power. You haven't claimed it yet."

I don't respond. I can't. My throat closes with the weight of it all.

"I nearly destroyed myself before I realized the truth," she continues. "That strength doesn't come from bloodline or birthright. We have to choose to access it. We have to open ourselves up to it and let it flow through us."

I glance sideways at her, skeptical of her words.

"I chose to believe I was strong," she says. "And so I became strong."

Her eyes find mine.

"And now, you must too."

I shake my head, a tremor of fear slithering down my spine. "I don't know how."

"You do," she says. "But you're still waiting for someone to hand you an instruction manual. You're waiting for someone to tell you that you're good enough. But nothing anyone says will ever make that true until you believe it's true."

I bristle at her words, but I can't deny that she's caught me out. I think about trying to erect a barrier around my dog, Duchess's, treat. It wasn't so long ago, but it feels like a lifetime ago. I had no confidence in myself at all back then. I thought that my power would never manifest fully until I found my One.

And then there were Four of them, each bringing out something new in me. Even then, I felt like a freak. I felt like all of this, the war and chaos on Altinna's shore, were because of me. And, maybe it is. But Seraphira is right. No one else is coming to save me. No one else is coming to save Altinna. If I can't do it, who will?

I turn my attention back to her Four, still mesmerized by how in sync they are. Is it because they love her? Because she loves them? Or, maybe, is it because they know that their true purpose is to lead as one?

They each have their own strengths, sure, but they have one purpose. One of them wields fire, while another manipulates the wind to spread the fire far and wide, blazing through their enemies. The third shakes the world with each and every one of his steps. When he moves, the enemies fall into cracks in the ground. Finally, the last fae wields power as intangible as the moonlight. The space around him bends and changes, warping at his will.

Each one of Seraphira's Four is powerful in his own right, but it's only because they work together, because they work at her command, that they are able to work as one. I watch as they decimate the enemies standing on the battlefield.

But that alone isn't enough. I know the legends. Altinna's enemies were ruthless and as numerous as the stars. It wasn't until the barrier was erected that they were finally able to succeed. Still, it was these four fae and Seraphira who erected the barrier. It was their deep trust of themselves and of each other that allowed them to access such powerful magic.

"They stood with me," she says, as if reading my mind. "Even when they were afraid. Even when they weren't sure they could win."

I glance at her. "But you did win."

Her eyes flick to mine, a hint of impatience in them. "Only because I stopped doubting myself. And once I stopped doubting myself and allowed the power in, we had the strength we needed to conquer."

A silence falls between us. The distant clash of weapons and magic hums through the air like a heartbeat, steady and terrible.

"You're not as different from me as you think," Seraphira continues. "You already have everything you need."

I press a hand to my chest, but the heaviness there hasn't lifted. "I'm not strong enough, not without all of them. Akin is gone. How am I supposed to go on without all of them?"

Her mouth presses into a hard line, and her eyes soften. "You think power only lives in numbers?"

"No," I say, my voice brittle. "But it's supposed to live in the balance of our connection. I had four, and now there are three."

"Your love for him transcends death and loss, Maerilee. It doesn't matter if he's gone. You still have everything you need to save Altinna. The time is coming very soon when you will need to restore the barrier. You will have to do it with or without Akin."

I stare at her, my mouth dry. "I don't know if I can do it without him."

Seraphira's silver eyes hold mine, bright and ancient and wild. "Then wake up," she says. "Wake up and find out what you're capable of."

The moment the words leave her mouth, the world shatters around me. I wake with a gasp. My whole body jerks upright, sweat slick across my skin, my breath ragged and shallow. The room is silent, cast in slanted moonlight. The fire has burned low in the hearth. My blankets are half-kicked to the floor.

I sit completely still.

The dream or vision, or whatever it was, still clings to me like static. Every part of me hums with power. My fingertips tingle. My spine thrums like a struck chord. Something has changed inside of me. It's like the power is flowing on its own accord.

I think of Seraphira's words. I have to let the power in. I close my eyes and feel it coursing within me, imagine it outside of me. I speak to it like it's a living entity, and maybe it is.

"I need you," I say, and I feel it respond, feel it crash over me like a wave.

I swing my legs over the edge of the bed, then pause, pressing a hand flat to my chest. The ache I've carried since Akin fell is still there. But now it pulses, alive. It's not the echo of loss anymore. It's the echo of something returning.

I stand, fast and light, and don't even bother dressing. I just pull a robe around my shoulders and fling the door open, barefoot in the cold hall. I have to find my mother and tell her what's happening to me. She, more than anyone else, will understand. She'll know what to do.

I don't know what I'm going to say, but I need to see her face. I need her to look at me and tell me if I've gone mad or if something in me has finally woken up. Then I need to find River, Brook, and Permiton. There's no time left for us to wait.

We have to save Altinna. Now.

HOPE RETURNED

The gates to the castle burst open for the four of us. I push through first, my sword still drawn, the metallic echo of steel on stone ringing through the courtyard like thunder. The guards barely have time to part before I'm through, their startled shouts falling behind me as I stride across the threshold, boots pounding against the cold, polished floor.

Brook and Permiton are right behind me, one arm slung over each of their shoulders, with Akin between them, barely standing, swaying with every step, but alive. He's more than a little beaten up, his strength completely zapped. But that's why we're here.

We don't know how, but he's here. One moment, we were standing in an apparently empty ruin, feeling like all hope was gone. The next, Akin appeared before us, like magic. In fact, probably because of magic. But Permiton kept muttering that it wasn't possible, that no ordinary fae could have broken through shadow magic like that.

I've known for quite a while that Akin was no ordinary fae, but I never expected that he'd have such powerful magic. If he weren't so banged up, he'd probably be laughing about it or telling us that magic is an overrated way to cheat the system.

What matters now, though, is that he is alive. He's alive and he's within the thinly held barrier. Still, my jaw is clenched so tight it hurts. I don't lower my sword. Not yet. Not until I know he's completely safe from Eirliwyn's shadow magic. The queen will know what to do. She'll know how to keep him from further harm.

The soldiers in the hall gape at us as we pass. A few bow, but most just stare in complete shock. Let them. I don't care anymore. Every part of me is focused on one thing–getting him to Queen Kimalissa.

We make it halfway through the front hall when Maerilee appears. I spot her at the same moment Akin does. She's walking fast at first, her eyes focused in the way I know they do when she's got a mission on her mind. She pays us no attention at first, wherever she's going her only priority.

But then, Akin whispers her name. She stops, turns to us, and freezes in place.

Her face goes completely pale and her body still. Her eyes are wide. Shock ripples across her face. For a heartbeat, she just stares, like she's trying to make sense of the ghost in front of her.

We all hold our breaths, waiting to see her reaction. This will either shake her from the daze she's been in, or completely break her.

A silence falls between all of us.

Then, she's running. Not a dignified rush or queenly stride, but a desperate, full speed, heart-first, no hesitation kind of run.

"Akin," she breathes, skidding to a stop in front of him.

Her hands go to his face first, trembling as they touch his cheeks, his jaw, brushing aside a lock of dark, sweat-dampened hair. Then his shoulders. His arms. His chest.

She doesn't hug him. Not yet.

She checks him, feeling him, searching for answers, making sure he's real. After everything she's been through, naturally, she needs to know he's not a trick or another illusion conjured by exhaustion and grief.

Tears spill over her lashes, silent and unchecked, the moment she realizes that it really, truly, is Akin. His knees buckle slightly, and Permiton and Brook tighten their hold. He offers her a crooked grin, his lips cracked, his face pale, but the light in his eyes is unmistakable.

"You look like hell," he rasps.

Her lips tremble.

And then she smacks his arm. Hard.

"You ass!" she cries. "I watched you die!"

Akin laughs, hoarse and sharp, and nearly collapses again. Brook catches him. I move in instinctively, bracing his other side.

"Not even death could keep me away from you, my love," he answers with full sincerity.

Maerilee throws her arms around him, finally pulling him close, holding onto him like the world might disappear again if she lets go. And for the first time in weeks, her shoulders shake not with rage or terror, but with something like relief.

I glance at Permiton. He's pale and shaking too, his knuckles white where he grips Akin's arm, but his eyes are locked on Maerilee. He blinks once, hard, like he still can't believe what he's seeing.

Brook turns his face away, but I see the tears clinging to his lashes. Meanwhile, I feel still in a way I haven't in weeks. Akin is here, and now we finally have a chance. It's taken so long. With him brought back to life, Maerilee can find the strength to survive.

We all can.

After a moment of a sweet reunion that we all shield our eyes from, she turns from Akin, her arms still trembling from the effort of holding him, and looks at the rest of us. There's something in her eyes I haven't seen in a long time, something alive. Something fierce.

She moves toward me first, and I brace myself, not sure what she's going to do. She throws her arms around me and hugs me hard, her tears brushing against my tunic.

"Thank you," she whispers into my shoulder. "For bringing him back."

I blink, caught off guard. My hands rise to her back, slow and unsure at first. Then I let myself hold her. Just for a breath. Just for this one perfect second. When she pulls away, her lips find mine, soft and quick, like fire or lightning. And then she releases me, giving Permiton and Brook each a heartfelt hug and kiss, expressing her thanks and her profound love for each of us.

She steps back after that, her eyes glassy but her shoulders squared like steel beneath her dress.

"I want to know everything," she says, voice low but urgent. "How you found him. How you got him out. How he's even still alive."

I open my mouth to answer, but the moment I do, the floor shifts beneath our feet. A deep, violent shudder rolls through the stone, rattling the stained-glass windows above us. Dust falls from the archways. Somewhere down the hall, a vase crashes to the ground and shatters, and in the distance, we hear the war horns blare. The sound pierces the air like a scream. Every muscle in my body goes taut.

"No," Maerilee whispers, terrified.

I turn and bolt for the front doors, yanking one open just enough to peer outside. All around the kingdom, it's like the sky is on fire. The barrier is evaporating, its shimmer of magic burning up until it's completely gone.

The Oceanan army and Diereken's forces are advancing toward the castle, all one unit. Our last hope is the hastily formed barrier that Maerilee placed around the castle. Not that I doubt Maerilee's abilities, but it was always meant to be a last resort. It's doubtful that it's going to hold under the weight of a full attack.

Their banners fly high. Their weapons gleam. Their war cries rise as the ground continues to shake, partly from the barrier falling, and partly from the massive number of soldiers advancing toward us.

I turn to see Maerilee stumbling to my side, her hand gripping the doorframe. Her face is as pale as I've ever seen it, horror in her eyes.

"Oh gods," she breathes.

"We have to go," I tell her, grabbing her and pulling her back toward the hallway where we left the others. "We have to get you somewhere safe. I don't know how long the castle's barrier is going to last."

"I made it in grief," she murmurs. "In shock. I didn't even know what I was doing. It's going to fall."

Behind us, Brook's voice cuts in, urgent. "What the hell is going on out there?"

"The barrier is falling, isn't it?" Permiton asks, his face ashen. "We have to get Maerilee away from here."

"It'll be a siege," Akin finishes, voice low and ragged. "And we're not prepared."

Maerilee turns sharply toward him, then to us. Her face is pale, but her eyes burn.

"I'm not leaving my people!" she screams. "My safety doesn't matter if my subjects are dead. We have to find a way to save everyone."

A new voice joins us. My spine stiffens even before I turn. Queen Kimalissa enters the hall, flanked by two guards, her silver hair loose around her shoulders, her robe half-tied like she'd dressed in a rush. Her face is grim, but determined.

"It's now or never," she says, her gaze locked on Maerilee. "You have to re-erect the barrier."

Maerilee flinches.

"What if I'm not strong enough?" she asks, shaking like a leaf.

Queen Kimalissa looks at her compassionately, then turns her attention to the rest of us.

"You'll need full access to your powers," she says decisively. "We're going to have to complete the binding ceremony. Right now."

BOUND

There's no time to think, no time to question or wonder if this is right or fair. No matter what happens after, we have to act now. We rush through the halls with Mother at the front guiding us, our footsteps echoing against the stone as if the castle itself is awake and holding its breath.

I can feel my Four are at my side.

River is like a storm held tight in a bottle, broody and dangerous. Brook's quiet strength pulses at my back, steady and sure. Permiton moves with the purpose of an ancient wisdom. Akin is unbelievably alive again, raw and radiant.

I think of Seraphira's Four again. The vision of them I saw what feels like just moments ago. They became a singularity, a functioning group rather than five individuals. If we have any hope of re-erecting the barrier, that is what we must become. And this binding ceremony will be the final piece to make that happen.

We burst into the throne room, where everything is still, despite the war waging outside. We have a little time as long as my barrier holds, but there's no telling how long that will be. Still, what's about to happen here is sacred and ancient. Fae have been bound here for centuries, but I will be the first fae since Seraphira to be bound to Four. There's no telling what will happen, but I know that everything is about to change implicitly.

I hold onto Seraphira's words as my Four and I take our place in front of the throne. I have to choose to be strong. I have to choose to believe that I have the power to re-erect the barrier. Before, I didn't think I was strong enough to do any of this, but Seraphira reminded me that I am. She couldn't have known that Akin would somehow return from the dead, could she? No, she believed in my power. So now I have to choose to believe in it too.

My father and siblings are already there waiting for us, their eyes wide with both fear and awe. The golden throne gleams in the early morning light. My heart beats rapidly in my chest, with a mixture of fear and anticipation.

Mother turns to face us, her expression unreadable. She is not just my mother now. She is the queen of Altinna. It is her sacred duty to perform this ritual. Once we're bound, we sacrifice our wants and needs to each other wholly. We will not be able to forsake one another for the rest of our lives.

Most importantly, our powers will be merged. Whatever strength we have, we now share. We will all be able to access it.

"Are you ready?" Mother asks.

This isn't how I saw my binding happening. It's meant to be a much more formal affair. It usually takes weeks or months of preparation. For a royal fae, it's accompanied by a parade and days of celebration and festivity. Of all the things this war has robbed from us, though, a formal binding ceremony seems like the least of my problems.

I'm not sure if I'm ready, but I know that I'm willing. This is what it takes to save Altinna, and I love each of my Four. I look to Akin, who I thought was dead for so long. My love for him burned so brightly, it nearly paralyzed me when I thought he was lost to me forever. I used to believe he was my One, and that made me so incredibly happy. I would not want to embark on this journey without him.

Then I look at Permiton, and I know that my love for him burns just as brightly. Permiton is strange and stilted in many of his ways, but he's always sacrificed for me. He's put his life on the line for all of us once before. I love him for his selflessness and for the quiet way he loves me. I know that my future is safe with him.

Brook breathes steadily, and I feel like I'm looking at him for the first time in ages. He's changed so much since our journey to Bright Waters. He's stepped into more of a leadership role, and most importantly, he stepped up when I was falling apart. He cares for me so deeply, and I want to spend my life making sure he knows how much I see him and love him.

Finally, there's River, his jaw tight with tension. But it isn't the same kind of tension it used to carry. He used to use his royalty as a shield, a way to manipulate others and get what he wanted. He was so entitled and arrogant, willing to hurt others to get what he wanted. But when he chose to stay with me, he proved his allegiance. Ever since that day, he's changed into a man who has compassion and kindness. I can hardly believe it, but I've grown to love him in a way that is just as raw and passionate as he is.

I cannot imagine my life without any of them. And if the barrier should fall and our enemies strike us all down, I want to die with them. That is enough for me to go through with this.

"I'm ready," I say.

Mother nods. "Then let us begin."

She steps back and gestures toward the center of the room.

"There," she says. "On the ancient seal."

I look down.

The floor of the throne room is cut with a massive circle of ancient stonework I've seen my whole life but never paid much attention to. Now, the runes carved into the stone pulse faintly with gold light, the pattern shifting, almost breathing, like it's alive and realizes what's about to happen.

I walk into the center, the stone warm beneath my feet. The others move to follow.

"Wait," my mother says, holding up a hand. "The Four must

surround her. Equal parts protection and power. This is not about one guarding the rest. This is about being one."

The four men pause, exchanging glances.

Then they move, fluid and sure, forming a loose circle around me.

Mother steps forward, her hands lifted, her voice softer now. "River and Permiton, take her left hand together. Brook and Akin, her right."

They do.

River's fingers are warm and steady. Permiton's are cold and trembling, but they curl firmly around mine.

On the other side, Brook's palm is slightly damp, but he tightens his grip without hesitation. Akin's hand is solid, sure, grounding.

Their fingers link across mine. And then, one by one, they reach out for each other. Akin clasps River's hand, River clasps Brook's, Brook clasps Permiton's, and Permiton clasps Akin's. The circle is complete.

My breath catches as a hum begins beneath my feet. The runes flare to life, golden and ancient, threading outward from the seal and lacing around the chamber in delicate veins of magic. Mother steps back and raises her arms, beginning to chant.

The words are old, older than any I've ever heard. Some don't even sound like words at all, just resonant syllables that seem to vibrate in my chest. The air thickens. The light grows warmer, richer, suffusing everything in a golden glow. It wraps around our joined hands. Around our feet. Around our hearts.

The chamber trembles, not from the war outside, but from the power being drawn from within. My eyes flutter shut. And then I feel the love of my Four. Brook's steady devotion. Permiton's brilliant, burning mind. River's fierce, protective heat. Akin's loyalty like iron, unbreakable.

Their magic rushes through me, and mine rushes back into them. We're not just touching. We're fused together, as if by iron.

I open my eyes and see their expressions changing, simultaneously softening and sharpening. Akin's skin shimmers faintly, light glowing beneath the surface like morning breaking through stone.

Brook's eyes glow deep sea blue, his shoulders drawing back with confidence. Permiton's hair lifts slightly on a breeze that isn't there, the space around him warping subtly, vision sparking behind his irises. River's jaw tightens, his chest rising, hands glowing with heat and clarity.

Mother's voice rises, reaching a crescendo. The light explodes, but it isn't blinding. It's revealing. In that one glorious moment, I feel what it is to be whole. I'm not alone anymore. I am fully and completely bound to these men. Together, we are something more than the sum of our parts.

We are divine.

Mother stands just outside the circle, the light of the runes casting her in an ethereal glow. Her shoulders are drawn back, her spine straight, her face steady and sure. But her eyes give away her pride… also her fear.

The war still rages outside. I can feel it in the tremble of the stone, in the way the barrier pulses like a failing heartbeat. If, for some reason, this doesn't work, all is lost. But it will work. I choose to believe it. I choose to accept their power and their love.

Mother raises her chin and speaks.

"Once this is done, you will no longer be separate. Your fates will be intertwined beyond what any magic has bound before. The pain of one will be the pain of all. The power of one, shared by all. There will be no turning back."

Her gaze lands on me first. Then shifts slowly, deliberately, to each of the four men beside me.

"Do you accept this?"

She looks to Permiton first. His eyes are clear, wide, his mouth parted slightly in reverent awe. He sees more than the rest of us, and still, he nods.

"I accept," he says softly. "I accept you."

Brook's fingers tighten around mine next. He doesn't look nervous now. Just open, raw, and full of emotion so intense it makes my knees weak.

"I've never wanted anything more," he murmurs. "Yes."

Akin smiles. Even after everything, even after death, his eyes shine.

"You're everything," he whispers. "Always yes."

I turn to River last. He meets me with a slight smirk, like he's trying to be the cocky prince he used to be. But it falters quickly, revealing the truth in his expression. In it I see love, fear, and so much hope.

"I would bind myself to you a thousand times over," he says. "Yes."

I look at each of them, my Four, and know there's only one answer left to give.

"Yes," I say. "I accept all of you."

Mother's voice is solemn and powerful when she speaks the final words. "Then let it be done." The moment the last syllable leaves her mouth, the floor beneath us erupts.

Magic explodes from the center of the circle, raw and blinding. I cry out, not in pain, but in overwhelm. It pours into me, through me, and I can feel it weaving us together. Golden light flares from Akin, deep and grounded like the roots of a mountain. Silver wind spirals from Permiton, shimmering and sharp and filled with knowledge I can't comprehend. A current of deep blue rolls from Brook, soft and sure, steady as the tides. A burst of pure flame ignites from River, hungry but not destructive, fierce and protective and alive.

From me, white light pours forth, humming with all the magic passed down through my mother, and her mother before her. Through Seraphira. Through every queen Altinna has ever known.

The threads of light twist and weave around each other, not in chaos, but in unity. It braids together, binding us into one.

One heart. One magic.

My body trembles as I feel their magic settle into me, become part of me. And mine flows into them, tying us together, deeper than blood. We are no longer separate. We are no longer alone.

Then the light explode in such a brilliant flash, a wave of color so intense I can't keep my eyes open.

It surges outward, past the circle, through the room, down the corridors of the castle like a tidal wave of power. I feel it ripple outward, breaking through the lingering veil of shadow that has plagued this place for weeks. For months. Maybe for generations.

It cuts through the fear, through the lingering despair. It casts away the darkness. It seals us in. Not just the five of us, but my family, and the soldiers, and every resident of Altinna.

Everything goes deadly quiet. I feel my knees buckle. Someone shouts my name, several someones perhaps, but the sound is distant, echoing. My hands slip from theirs. My vision tilts.

The golden light fades from my skin, the glowing runes along my arms flickering like the last remnants of starlight before dawn, and then the ground rushes up to meet me.

I fall into arms, I think, but I'm already unconscious before I know whose.

THE ORIGINAL QUEEN

SERAPHIRA

The battlefield trembles beneath my feet, each pulse of the earth echoing like a heartbeat I can no longer ignore. Smoke coils in the air, thick with ash and blood and the remnants of what we've already lost. The cries of my people fade into the background as I stand at the center of it all, where past, present, and future converge.

This is the war I was born into, but it will not be the war I die in.

I close my eyes. Let the wind wrap around me, cool against the heat of my skin, let the magic beneath the surface of the land hum in my bones, let the voices of the fallen guide me.

My Four stand around me. They are my soul, my heart, and my strength.

Valen, with fire always burning behind his dark eyes, his passion wild and consuming, gives me courage like I've never known. Orienne, fierce and agile, the wind at his back, his breath tethered to every current that shifts the tides of battle, instills in me a sense of power. Thalos, unmoving as stone, his connection to the earth deeper than roots, deeper than blood, grounds me. And Elias, as always, is my light. His very presence bends the air, his magic like a soft halo around my soul.

They are with me in body, in spirit, and in magic. Their hands do not touch mine, but their power is laced into every breath I take. We are one, bound together forever.

I lift my arms to the sky. The wind stills. The earth quiets. Even the sun hesitates at the horizon, watching. The runes carved into the stones of this cursed field begin to glow, ancient markings only visible to those who remember what it means to wield the truth of the land. They light up beneath my feet first, then ripple outward, a pulse of golden magic that reaches toward the edges of the kingdom, stretching farther than even the eye can see.

Behind me, my people kneel, not in surrender, but in faith. Their faces are streaked with dirt, sweat, and blood, but their eyes are fixed on me, on us. Their belief is not blind. It is earned. They trust me to end this war, to protect them, to give them peace in a world that has only ever taught them to fight.

Thalos is the first to move. His hand drops to the cracked soil, fingers splayed wide, and I *feel* the shift as his power dives deep. The earth groans, ancient veins awakening, roots threading into the magic to anchor it, to hold it steady through whatever storms may come. The ground around us darkens, then solidifies, forming the foundation of what will become the great divide between peace and ruin.

Next comes Orienne. He closes his eyes, lifts his face to the sky, and calls to the wind. It answers him like a lover, swift and sure, wrapping around him and through him, weaving itself into the threads of the spell. It forms the frame, the breath of the barrier. Fast, free, impenetrable. It wraps around Thalos's foundation like silk over stone.

Valen steps forward. He says nothing. He never does at moments like this. His eyes meet mine, and that's all we need. He ignites. Flames spill from his palms, licking the edge of the circle, racing along the carved runes like a fuse. The magic doesn't burn but rather refines. It scorches away what's broken, what's weak, what would try to bend the barrier's will. Valen's fire is not meant to destroy, but to seal, to burn away the old world so a new one can rise in its place. The flames roar upward, dancing like wild serpents across the wind.

And then Elias steps into the circle. His hands glow with the same silvery light that shines from his eyes. His magic surges forward with a kind of divine stillness. It wraps the spell in certainty, in clarity, in love. It binds all that we have given and fuses it into something immortal.

And still I stand in the center. Still, I have not cast my part. Because mine is the last, the most difficult, the most permanent. I draw in a breath.

My body is shaking, not with fear, but with the weight of it all. The weight of legacy and lineage. Of the queens who came before me and the daughters who will come after.

I press my palm against my chest, against the place where their magic lives now, threaded through mine, and I speak.

"I am Seraphira of Altinna," I say, and my voice is not just mine, it is theirs. My Four. My people. My ancestors and my descendants. "And I call this place sacred. This land, this sky, this realm."

The runes pulse brighter. I fall to my knees.

"I bind this kingdom in light. I hold its heart in mine. I weave my soul into the bones of its foundation, and I offer my magic, freely and without condition, that it may live long after I am gone."

The wind howls. The flames rise. The earth trembles. And then the light, my light, bursts from my chest. It pours outward like a flood, weaving through every tendril of magic my Four have given, joining them into something whole, something eternal.

I scream, not in pain, but in effort, in release and in surrender. This is everything I have, everything I am. With my sacrifice of self, the spell completes. The barrier rises around the entire kingdom, strong and formidable.

I feel it the moment it snaps into place. It's a dome of pure, radiant force that stretches high above the battlefield and outward beyond the hills, past the mountains, through the forests.

Then there's silence. No more shouting. No more death cries. No more war. Just wind and peace, and the slow realization that we've done it.

I collapse to the ground, gasping. My Four rush to me, their faces filled with awe and terror and love. Valen gathers me into his arms. Orienne presses his hands to my face. Thalos steadies my spine, his grounding presence keeping me from floating away. Elias kneels beside me, his light already mending the pieces of me I didn't know had broken.

"You did it," Elias whispers, eyes wet. "You *did* it."

But I shake my head. We did it, all of us together, and now Altinna is protected by the force of our love. Our magic is not woven for war, but for peace and prosperity.

If my descendants ever find themselves lost in the dark again, I pray this barrier will remember what it means to stand in the light.

Our enemies scream in frustration and pain. Our barrier has pushed them all outside of our dome of perfect peace. They see it, strike it, throw their magic, their arrows, their rage at the glowing shield, but it holds. They beat their fists against it. They cast darkness, summon storms, call forth every monstrous creature they can, but none of it passes through. The barrier does not waver, and it never will.

I lower my arms slowly. My body trembles. My muscles burn with the ache of a thousand lifetimes compressed into a single heartbeat. Sweat rolls down my spine. My vision blurs. But I stay standing, fueled by the relief that it is done. The war is over now. There will be peace.

At last, I exhale. The breath is shaky, but it feels like the purest I've ever breathed. The air feels fresher, finally clear of the smoke that's plagued us for so many years.

Behind me, my Four move closer. Valen's hand settles against my back. Orienne brushes a lock of hair from my face. Thalos steadies my shoulder. Elias presses his forehead to mine, his magic still a quiet hum that promises I am not alone. I am never alone.

The field is still. A gentle wind blows across the scorched grass.

It carries with it the scent of rain, of renewal, the promise of something new.

And then, just as I start to turn toward my people, toward the future we will build from this scorched earth, I see an unfamiliar young woman standing on a hill in the distance.

She stands just beyond the edge of the battlefield, half in shadow, half in light. Her hair glints silver-white. Her eyes are wide, luminous, filled with sorrow and awe, and of an ancient recognition.

She does not belong to this time, but she belongs here, to this land. I step toward her slowly.

The world shifts around her, blurring at the edges, like she is not fully formed, like she stands in the seam between dreams and memory, a crack in the fabric of magic, a ripple through time. In the blink of an eye, she is no longer far from me, but standing right in front of me, her face full of fear and doubt.

I know her. I know her heart. I feel the tether between us. Not born of blood, but of purpose.

"You," I whisper.

She swallows hard. "You just erected the barrier for the first time?" she asks in awe, a little breathless.

A smile tugs at my lips. I reach for her cheek, but my hand passes through as if she's made of smoke and moonlight.

"I did," I say softly. "And now it is your turn."

She shakes her head, tears blurring in her eyes. "Why me?" she asks.

I study her. The glint of power barely hidden in her bones. The cracks of grief are still raw in her soul. The love braided around her like armor. Her raw, unfiltered magic crackles through it, and I feel it crackling through me as well.

We are of one line. She is my descendant, blood of my blood. The moment the barrier locked into place, her thread ran through it. A piece of her always lived here.

"Because you are the beginning again," I whisper. "Because you will stand where I stood. Because the world will need you, as it once needed me."

She shakes her head again, breath catching. "We don't have the same kind of power," she says, looking beyond me toward my Four.

"What you just did was nothing short of magnificent, but we're not the same. You're all so much stronger."

"Maerilee, it is the love you share that makes you powerful. You don't need the same exact powers because the love you share is just as strong as ours. But remember this, my daughter. You are not whole because of them. But with them, you are unstoppable."

I motion toward where I feel her Four waiting just beyond the veil.

"I don't want to go," she says.

"You must."

"I'm not ready. I don't know what waits for me when I wake back up to reality."

"Your future awaits, Maerilee. I feel it in my bones. Altinna does not fall because of you. It becomes much stronger than I could ever make it."

She looks down. "Will I see you again?"

I tilt my head, considering.

"Perhaps not as I am," I say. "But I will never leave you."

The wind picks up again, carrying her away, scattering her form like petals on a current.

And just before she's gone, she whispers, "Thank you."

When I blink, she is gone. Only the empty battlefield remains, a reminder that we have much rebuilding to do. We have defeated our enemies, finally, but now it is up to us to shape the future of Altinna. What we decide now will affect the Altinna that Maerilee will live in one day.

In spite of the weight of this knowledge, the air feels lighter around us. The future feels closer than it ever has. Most importantly, we know that we have a future. We will negotiate our enemies' surrender. We will broker a peace that will last for centuries. We will create a kingdom that is protected by a deep and ancient love.

And, one day, when that protection becomes eroded with greed and shadow and ego, I know Maerilee will be there with her Four, to push it back and build an even stronger foundation. Altinna will stand longer than any of us.

A NEW ALTINNA

MAERILEE

The Oceanan army has breached the gates of our kingdom now that the barrier is down. We watch from above as their forces pour into the city, clashing with what remains of our warriors.

Splintered wood and twisted metal lie strewn across the marble road like bones of a fallen titan. The Oceanans pour through the breach like a tide long held at bay. Steel flashes in the sun. Magic explodes in the air, shards of ice, jets of water, bolts of sky fire. The scent of blood clings to the wind, mixing with the acrid tang of smoke. Screams rise above the chaos, but I don't flinch. I'm not afraid anymore.

I can tell by their posture that our enemies think they have won. But they don't know yet what's happened. They don't know their fates are sealed.

We fly down to the edge of the barrier, the gold of our wings catching the sunlight and glinting onto the battlefield. I had barely felt my wings in the moments after the binding ceremony, just a strange pull, a tingle along my back. But a moment after I came to from my vision of Seraphira, the five of us took off, through the skylights of the throne room.

We took the briefest moment to survey the scene, to see what we were up against as we mounted our final battle. But it doesn't matter what our enemies throw at us now. I've seen the past. I've spoken to Seraphira. I know what I must do, what we all must do.

To my left, Akin stands tall, his obsidian wings sharp and sleek, the wind tugging at his tunic as his eyes sweep the battlefield like a soldier gauging his next strike. To my right, River's wings are the color of deep, angry storms. They shift with energy, crackling faintly as his fists curl at his sides. The fire in him burns steady now, no longer a threat but a force I can trust.

Brook is behind me, his silvery-blue wings broad and curved like waves in mid-crash, his hands already glowing with icy water, ready to defend. Permiton's wings shimmer with shifting light, like the veil between realms. He stares through the barrier, not at the soldiers, but beyond them, once again seeing more than what's visible.

Their presence strengthens me, fills in every fracture that once existed. I can feel them in my blood, their power braided into mine. I feel River's control, Brook's depth, Akin's strength, Permiton's Sight. I draw on them as easily as breathing. A sense of calm radiates through me like nothing I've ever experienced before. I'm not sure if it's Sight or just confidence, but I know without a doubt that we're on the verge of winning this war.

Diereken stalks toward the barrier like a lion approaching prey, his army spreading out behind him. He's tall, cloaked in midnight armor that glints with dark enchantment. His eyes blaze with cruel amusement. He lifts his hands and claps, mockingly slow.

"Well done, Princess," he calls, his voice curling like smoke across the scorched courtyard. "I see you've completed your unnatural binding ceremony with your Four. You bought yourself time, but that's all you've done."

I walk toward him, each step deliberate and calm. My boots click softly against the cracked stone, the wind tugging at my hair, at my wings. The barrier flickers as I approach it, waiting for me to command it. I understand now. It isn't just my magic. It's my being. It responds to me because it trusts me.

I stop a breath away from the edge. Diereken smiles again, smug and condescending.

"You're shaking," he sneers, though that couldn't be farther from the truth. "The moment this barrier falls, I'm cutting off your head and keeping it as my prize."

I tilt my head, filled with an apathetic disgust I never expected to feel standing so close to him.

"You're mistaken," I tell him. "You are the one trembling."

Then I lift my hand and take one step forward.

The barrier pulses and expands, rippling outward like a living force. Diereken stumbles back, caught off guard. His sneer falters, replaced by confusion, then rage.

"You—" he snarls.

But I smile as I tap into the ancient power that isn't just within me. It's in the earth. In the roots of Altinna. In the rivers, the mountains, the sky. It always has been. My ancestors merely held the key. Seraphira whispered it into my bones. My Four unlocked it.

I close my eyes and reach downward, not with my hands, but with my soul. And the kingdom answers me. Magic erupts from the very stones beneath my feet. Light bursts from my chest, surging skyward. It blinds everyone on the battlefield. I hear screams. I hear gasps. But none of it touches me. The wind howls, not in protest, but in exaltation.

The runes carved into the bones of Altinna blaze to life. The barrier reforms, no longer temporary. No longer fragile. It grows. It expands from the throne room, the palace walls, from the very center of Altinna and rushes outward. The magic spins in gold and white and blue, threaded with the essence of my Four, with the ancient forces Seraphira once called upon. It curves like a dome, encompassing the kingdom in a single, unbreakable force.

Diereken screams as he's forced backward by the force of the magic. He strikes at it with all his power, with spells of shadow, blades of parasitic magic, twisted curses hurled from his outstretched hands. But nothing even touches it. The barrier doesn't tremble. It sings.

And in that moment, he realizes it's over. The magic rushes

toward him like a crashing tide. He stumbles, roars, tries to flee, but the light is faster. It wraps around him, not gently. This is not the peace of healing. This is justice that has waited too long, the kind that cannot be undone.

The barrier consumes him, exposing his every truth. It strips him bare, shatters his illusions, and unweaves the foul magic he's stolen from other kingdoms. And then he is gone in a flash of brilliant white.

The soldiers left behind falter. I feel the moment the last of them touch the edge of the barrier and are forced out. They are not killed like he was, but they are permanently banished. I feel the finality of it, of the barrier's decision of who can and cannot enter my kingdom.

I sway on my feet, dizzy from the magic's intensity, from the sheer finality of it. Akin is beside me in an instant, catching me by the waist.

"It's done," I whisper, my voice raw.

He nods, pressing his forehead to mine. "You did it."

"No," I say, smiling as the glow fades from my skin. "*We* did."

A beat passes. The battlefield is silent now, save for the wind. The remnants of the Oceanan and Ambrosian armies are now relegated to the edges of the barrier, unable to cross into Altinna ever again until I give them permission.

But there's one enemy who does not deserve simple banishment. A coldness creeps across my skin as I remember him, as I think about the way he slipped past our defenses before and used his dark magic to make me think I was losing my mind, how he used his shadows to still Akin from me.

He's no longer in the kingdom, also pushed out by the strength of my new barrier, but we will find him. We will bring him to justice.

He deserves no less than the cruelest fate.

Akin

. . .

Since waking from the shadows, there's been a quiet thrum inside me, like a second heartbeat, a pulse beneath the skin, not quite pain, not quite power. At first, I thought it was a trick of the dark magic that held me captive, a residue, a cruel reminder that I had been used.

But now I know better. What I'm feeling was not given to me because of the darkness. No, it was always living inside of me, but Eirliwyn's attack awakened it and forced it out of me. This light, this powerful force inside of me, is a direct attack to his dark magic. I don't know what to call it. I don't know very much about magic. But I know it's powerful and ancient, and that we can use it to finally bring that bastard to justice.

Once the barrier was erected, once we celebrated and I got to reunite with my love properly, I finally tell the others about it.

"When I was bound in darkness, it was like a force pushing out against it," I explain to them in the war room, trying to find the words. "You all started to leave me, and it's like it exploded out of me. It got rid of the darkness, and that's when you were able to see me."

Permiton confirms it first. He stands in front of me, staring, then says simply, "Your bloodline carries light magic. You were born with it, Akin. But it's been dormant. Your family must have buried it long ago, hidden it. Perhaps they even feared it."

And when he says that, I see it, the way I can see everything now. The Sight flickers through me in brief, brilliant flashes, borrowed through the bond we share. I see the generations before me, stoic warriors, battle-hardened leaders. I see one man, centuries ago, standing beneath the stars with light pouring from his palms like water, a circle of people watching in awe. I see how that power dwindled over time, tucked away in favor of strength and steel.

But it's in me and it's awake now. It now flows through all of us, another line of defense that we didn't have before. I glance down at my hands. I don't need runes or symbols to know what's there. It shines beneath my skin, waiting to be wielded.

Days have passed since Maerilee re-erected the barrier, and we have spent most of them trying to decide what to do about Eirliwyn.

With Diereken dead, his forces have retreated to Ambrosia, and a small band of our soldiers has gone forth with a message from Maerilee.

They are banished from Altinna forever, unless their king and queen agree to a peace treaty. Should the treaty ever be broken, fire will rain down from Altinna like nothing ever before it. By the time it reaches them, word will have spread of the barrier. Every kingdom will know of the extraordinary power we now possess.

Maerilee commanded that Commander Heela be arrested and kept in the dungeon until such a time that we can decide what to do with him. She's decreed that Brook and River be the ones to decide his punishment, once they speak to their parents and make it clear how formidable the five of us are now that we're bound.

As our enemies and allies alike become aware of what's happened here, there is just the matter of Eirliwyn. He is our only enemy born from inside these walls, his bitterness growing and blooming from the rejection of Queen Kimalissa. We've decided that once we find him, it will be her honor to execute him. Finding him, though, proves to be our biggest challenge.

Brook is the one who senses it first. He nudges me as we stand in the war room, the map of Altinna still glowing faintly with Seraphira's mark. "Your wings," he says.

I look over my shoulder. They've shifted. They used to be dark, shadowy like obsidian. But now, they shimmer faintly at the edges like moonlight on metal.

"They were darker," he murmurs. "Right after we were bound."

I nod. "I know."

River crosses his arms. "So what does it mean?" he asks, his impatience etched on his face.

Maerilee rolls her eyes at him, though it's in fondness.

Permiton steps forward. "Maybe it means that Eirliwyn's shadow magic is still somehow part of you, Akin," he says, sounding strangely hopeful. "Maybe that means we can use your light magic to find him."

His Sight wraps around my light magic now, overlapping like two hands folded together. He doesn't have to point. I can see the rail of shadow magic curling through the castle grounds.

He's hiding, deep below the castle, in the dungeons beneath the west wing, tucked in the bones of the palace where no sunlight reaches. He has probably been there from the beginning, using his shadow magic to coordinate with our enemies from his seclusion. His reign ends now.

We descend slowly. I take the lead. The corridors grow darker, narrower. The magic in me brightens in response, illuminating the stone walls, revealing ancient markings I've never noticed before.

"I didn't know these were here," River mutters.

"They've always been here," Permiton answers softly. "But only light reveals them."

We reach the final door. It creaks open without resistance. He's sitting in the center of the room, as though he were waiting for us.

His face is drawn, pale. The illusion of immortality is gone. His eyes flick up to me, and he smirks.

"You're a difficult man to kill," he says.

"So are you," I reply, stepping forward.

Brook stays at my right, River at my left, Permiton behind me, and Maerilee is sheltered between all of us. We surround him with our power. He doesn't move, though he probably thinks he can still take us.

"I'm surprised you found me," he says, almost impressed. "But I assure you, you won't be so lucky again."

He tries to once again disappear into smoke, but we're too fast for him. Maerilee erects a forcefield around him, stopping him from moving more than a few feet, even in his shadow form. I use my light magic to counteract his shadows, revealing him once again. Without his shadow magic, he's nothing more than a pitiful old man.

"Your arrogance makes you predictable," I say.

His smile fades, realizing he's been beaten. "I could've torn her apart," he mutters, quieter now. "She was already unraveling. If I'd had more time—"

"But you didn't," I cut in, my voice echoing in the chamber.

"Because she is stronger than you. And we are stronger together than you ever could be alone."

Something changes in his eyes then, not fear, but resignation. He knows this is the end. I hold out my hand. A ring of light surrounds him instantly, rising from the ground like smoke, then solidifying into a cage.

He hisses at it. "You don't even know how to use that magic—"

"I know enough," I say, cutting him off.

And I do. Because I don't need to be a master. I don't need decades of training or a library of spells. I just need my purpose.

And her.

We bring him to the throne room. It's the only place that feels right. Queen Kimalissa waits there, regal and still, King Fratino beside her, her silver crown catching the light. When she sees Eirlwyn, her lips press into a thin, pale line. For a moment, I think she might falter, but she stands, and her power returns, not her magic, but her authority.

"This man," she says, her voice sharp, ringing through the hall, "was once my advisor. Trusted. Valued. But he betrayed us. He sought to dismantle our kingdom from the inside, to sell us to our enemies, to destroy the one thing that binds us."

Her gaze falls to Maerilee, who moves to stand beside her mother, silent but steady.

"And for that," the Queen says, "he will be judged."

I unsheathe my sword, handing it to her, and then the four of us step back. This is her moment.

Queen Kimalissa rises from her throne, streaks of sunlight falling on her, making her look like she's glowing. Apt, considering she's about to exterminate this darkness once and for all. The king stays back, watching his wife with the pride and reverence she deserves.

Eirlwyn doesn't even try to fight. He looks at her like a man who already knows his sentence.

"Do you have anything to say for yourself?" she asks.

He lifts his chin. "You always chose wrong."

Her lips twitch. "No," she says. "I chose love."

She lifts the sword expertly, then plunges it swiftly into his heart through the bars of his cage. He crumples with the blade still in his chest. She doesn't bother to pull it out.

"I'll get you a new one," she tells me with a wink.

Maerilee steps forward and reaches for her mother's hand. They stand there, side by side, two queens. One past and one future. King Fratino stands, and the five of us encircle the two of them. For just one private moment, we allow ourselves to feel the relief.

It is finally over.

THE QUEEN OF ALL TIME

Maerilee

It's strange how quiet the castle feels now that the war is over. No battle cries echo off the walls. No generals bark orders in the courtyards. No smoke curls from the skyline. There's just the gentle hum of wind stirring the trees beyond the palace gates, the soft laughter of children somewhere in the gardens, and the sound of rebuilding.

Altinna is healing, and so am I.

The barrier stands again, stronger than before, more than magic now. It is memory, sacrifice, blood, and love. It is a promise sealed in fire and light. Sometimes, when I walk through the palace grounds, I feel it pulse faintly beneath my feet. As if it recognizes me. As if it knows that I am one of its keepers.

We all are. River, Brook, Akin, Permiton, and I. They aren't just my Four. They are my home.

It's been three months since Eirlwyn fell beneath my mother's judgment, since Diereken was consumed by the magic he thought he could bend... three months since we bound our souls in light and carved our future into the bones of the kingdom.

People still whisper about it. Some call it legend already. Others call it scandalous.

They still can't get over the fact that I was bound to four powerful fae. They believe it's unnatural, that it makes me unfit to lead. Thankfully, they have become a small minority, as many revere my Four for what they did to help in Altinna's time of need.

Those fae just call our union hope. We've given them something to believe in again.

My mother and father still rule, though they've offered me the throne more than once. My mother's voice shakes every time she makes the offer, like she wants to step back but also can't quite let go. And I understand. How could she not hesitate after everything?

So I told her no. Not yet. I want to let her reign a little longer while I figure out what it means to carry peace instead of war. I want her to stand tall in the spotlight while I adjust to sharing my life and my heart with four extraordinary, maddening, beautiful men.

Marriage is strange when it comes in fours.

I suppose it's not truly marriage in the traditional sense. There were no legal documents signed, no treaties formed. Just ancient magic, whispered words, and a binding spell so powerful that it lit up the entire kingdom.

We've been living in the royal wing ever since. Akin wakes up before dawn and trains in the courtyard, his new light magic glowing faintly around him as he adjusts to power he was never raised to wield. He grumbles about losing his edge, but he moves with more grace now, like he's become something more than a soldier, something brighter.

Brook spends his mornings in the library, combing through Oceanan battle texts and Altinnian history like a man possessed. He's still soft-spoken, but when he speaks, people listen. The generals come to him now for strategy. And he smiles a lot more. He's helping Akin to train young men so we can replenish our army.

Permiton paces constantly, jotting notes on parchment, obsessed with cataloging how our magic works now that we're bound. I don't think he's slept more than four hours in a row, but he swears he's never felt more alive. He's still as awkward as he ever was, but we've all grown to love his quirks.

River remains a walking contradiction, as always, smirking one moment, serious the next. He spends hours with the children we sheltered during the war. He reads to them in the sun, teaches them how to wield their water magic. I don't think even he realizes how many people admire him now… especially me.

I love them all, differently and deeply.

Completely.

Tonight, the five of us are being honored.

My mother has arranged a feast, lavish and ceremonial, with dancers and silk banners and imported wine. I didn't ask for it, but I'm not surprised. The people need a celebration, something beautiful to break the silence that followed the final battle. I need it, too.

The ballroom is draped in soft gold and violet. My family's colors. My future crown's colors. A new emblem has been added to the tapestries, five wings arched around a glowing star. It's the five of us, a quiet symbol of what we are now.

I stand near the window, fingers tracing the silver goblet in my hands, watching as guests fill the room… nobles, soldiers, ambassadors. Some are laughing. Some are whispering. But all of them look toward me when I enter.

It reminds me so much of that first ball where I was supposed to find my One. And, as if summoned by memory, he finds me.

"Planning your escape?"

River's voice slides against my ear, warm and amused. I turn, smiling despite myself.

"I was hoping no one would notice if I slipped out the window."

"Impossible," he murmurs, lifting my hand to his lips. "You're the most dangerous woman in the room."

"You're only saying that because I outrank you."

"Only technically," he whispers, but his smile deepens. "You're also terrifying. And stunning."

A flush creeps into my cheeks. "You're shameless."

"You married me," he replies smoothly.

"Technically, I married all of you."

He smirks. "Either way, I've won."

Before I can reply, a hand slips into mine from the other side. It's Brook.

"Don't let him rile you," he says gently, then he kisses my knuckles. "You look radiant tonight."

"Thank you," I breathe.

Akin appears next, his white tunic crisp against the golden light, wings tucked tight behind his back.

"We'll finally get to dance together in front of all the dignitaries," he says fondly, his eyes twinkling with love.

I think back to that same ball, where he had to stay at the edge of the ballroom, watching me with jealousy and fear that I would find someone else who would take me away from him.

"You will have my first dance," I promise him, pulling him in for a chaste kiss on the cheek.

Permiton arrives last, eyes flicking over all of us like he's still cataloging every moment.

"Princess," he greets casually, a slight smirk on his lips that rivals even Rivers. He's becoming a little bolder with his flirting. "The stars are all shining on you tonight, beloved."

I giggle helplessly, and the tension in my chest eases.

The music begins as my parents step onto the dais. My mother's dress sweeps the floor, silver hair braided with small gems. She looks every bit the ruler she is. She lifts her glass, her voice ringing clear.

"Tonight," she begins, "we celebrate not only the survival of our kingdom, but the rebirth of it. War has tested us. Loss has marked us. But we are still standing, stronger, brighter, and better than ever before."

The crowd quiets as she turns to me.

"To my daughter, Maerilee," she says, her voice wavering for only a second, "who bore the weight of this kingdom when even I could not, who faced darkness and chose to rise."

My throat tightens.

"And to the Four who stood with her," she continues, her eyes moving across Akin, Brook, Permiton, and River, "not just as warriors, but as soul-bound equals. As future leaders. As proof that love, no matter how unconventional, is the greatest magic we possess."

There's a murmur in the crowd, of agreement rather than dissent, much to my surprise and delight. She raises her glass higher.

"To Altinna's future. And to those who will lead it."

The crowd echoes the toast. I lift my own glass, my heart a storm of gratitude and disbelief. I didn't think I'd survive to see peace, but here I stand.

The music swells. The dance begins. I step into the light with my hand proudly in Akin's. We dance an old, ceremonial dance for newlyweds, but of course we don't dance long before River cuts in. Buoyed by his brother's arrogance and confidence, Brook quickly steps in. Finally, not to be left out, Permiton comes over and Brook gracefully moves out of the way for him.

And then the five of us are dancing together in a complicated jig that seems to flow from us as easily as our magic. I'm dancing with my husbands in celebration of our marriage and our victory.

It isn't unnatural. It's isn't wrong.

It's fate.

Permiton

The stars stretch across the sky in quiet celebration, soft glimmers scattered across the velvet dark. The halls are still glowing from the feast, lanterns swaying gently in the breeze, rose petals scattered on the floor where guests had once danced. Even the magic in the walls feels satisfied, like Altinna itself has exhaled.

But I can't sleep, and, apparently, neither can Maerilee.

She finds me in the library long after midnight, barefoot and still dressed in the silver-and-rose gown from earlier, her long hair braided loosely over one shoulder. She leans against the doorway, smiling like she's trying not to startle me.

"You're not tired?" she asks softly.

"Not even a little," I admit. "Though that's nothing new."

She walks to me without hesitation and slips into the chair across from mine. The fire crackles quietly between us, casting gold across her cheeks, her collarbones, her bare arms. I've been sitting here for over an hour with an open book in my lap and not a single line committed to memory.

She sighs. "I've been thinking."

I close the book gently. "Should I be worried?"

"Almost definitely," she teases. Then her face softens. "I keep remembering things, bits and pieces from Seraphira, from the dreams, or visions, or whatever they were."

I nod once, leaning forward. "Go on."

"She said I wasn't whole because of my Four," Maerilee murmurs. "But with you, I am unstoppable."

My throat tightens. "She was right."

"I think I can feel them sometimes," she continues, her voice almost reverent. "The rulers before me. Not just Seraphira. Others. Like they're reaching through time. Like they're watching me and supporting me."

I lean closer.

"You're connected to them. That's not surprising."

"But it doesn't feel like just a memory," she says, shaking her head. "It feels alive. Like I'm part of something much older than I ever realized."

"You are," I whisper.

We fall into a comfortable silence for a moment, and I let myself really study her. She's luminous in the firelight, but there's something else, deeper. Her silver eyes are alert and restless, her posture relaxed but never careless.

"How did it happen, Permiton?" she asks. "How did Seraphira pull me back into the moment the original barrier was erected?"

"I've been asking myself the same question," I admit. "And I've been researching."

"Of course you have," she says with a smile that curls around my ribs.

I clear my throat. "I believe your connection to the barrier, combined with our bond, opened a path through time. Not physical, of course, but a magical echo."

Maerilee leans forward. "So you think I didn't just dream it?"

"No." I meet her gaze. "I think you were there, in the way only magic can make possible."

She goes quiet, absorbing that. Then she whispers, "So what does that mean for the future?"

I hesitate. Because this is where my Sight once came easily. But now it only flickers, elusive and hazy around the edges. "I don't know," I say honestly. "But maybe you're not supposed to ask me anymore."

She blinks. "You think I'll be able to see the future, too?"

"Maybe not the way I do, or the way I did," I amend. "But something tells me this experience has given you more power than we know."

She shifts her weight in the chair, curling her legs beneath her, her eyes thoughtful. "I want to know everything," she says, "about time, the way it bends, the way you've seen it. I want to know what's possible."

I smile, a slow curve I don't think I ever used before she came into my life. "You might regret that," I say. "I can be a little overwhelming when I get excited."

"I like that about you," she says, and my heart stutters.

She moves again, this time sliding out of her chair and coming to sit beside me on the cushioned bench. Her thigh brushes mine. I try not to drop the book still balanced on my lap.

"I mean it," she says softly. "You fascinate me. The way your mind works. The way you see things others don't."

"I see you," I murmur.

She smiles and then leans in, her mouth brushing mine.

It's gentle at first. A soft invitation. But it deepens quickly, her fingers curling in the front of my shirt, her breath catching as she shifts to straddle my lap.

And suddenly I forget every theory I've ever had. My hands find her waist, sliding up the curve of her back as her lips move against mine. Her magic hums against my skin, not pressing, not overwhelming, just present, like she's offering it freely.

She pulls back just long enough to whisper, "We've never done it here."

My breath hitches. "The library?"

She nods, eyes sparkling. My head spins. On one hand, I'm already half-hard beneath her, her thighs framing mine, her mouth still hovering close enough to drive me mad. On the other hand....

"There are so many first editions in this room," I whisper.

She laughs and grinds against me.

"Don't worry, we won't hurt the books," she says, pressing a kiss beneath my jaw.

"I don't want to get kicked out of the royal archives," I say, groaning as her hands slide beneath my shirt. "That would be a tragic end to my legacy."

"You are the royal archives now," she teases.

I laugh, then gasp as she rocks against me again. My hands move without thought, sliding under her gown, pushing it up inch by inch until I find the soft skin of her thighs.

"Do you know how many times I imagined you like this?" I murmur. "Curled up beside me, asking impossible questions, and then...." I can't help but trail off.

"And then?" she breathes.

I slide a hand between us, cupping her over the silk beneath the gown. Her breath catches, her hips jerking toward me.

"And then unraveling," I whisper. "For me."

She doesn't answer. She just kisses me again, harder this time. She tugs at my shirt, and I let her, pulling it over my head and tossing it somewhere behind us, hopefully nowhere near the scrolls. Her hands trail across my chest, slow and searching, like she's memorizing every inch. Then her mouth follows.

I tilt my head back as her lips trace the curve of my neck, her teeth grazing lightly. I grip her hips, grounding myself in her body, her heat, her scent. The bond between us thrums to life, not magic, not exactly, but connection.

She leans back just enough to strip her gown over her head, revealing smooth skin and flushed cheeks and eyes that could split the world in half.

"I want to make you lose control," she says.

I lift her easily, spinning to lay her down on the chaise, careful to avoid the table of priceless journals nearby. She laughs again, breathless and wicked, and I swear I've never loved her more. I easily slip inside of her, like she was made specifically for me.

We move together in sync, each motion deliberate, slow at first, then faster, needier, tangled in limbs and gasps and whispered words that don't need to be recorded anywhere. Her legs wrap around me, her hands clutching my back as I push into her, filling her inch by inch until she gasps my name.

"Don't stop," she whispers.

"Never," I promise.

I lose myself in her.

In her rhythm. In her breath. In the way she shatters beneath me, body arching, mouth parting in a silent cry. And when I follow, it's with her name on my lips and stars behind my eyes.

We collapse together, tangled and panting, sweat cooling against fire-warmed skin. It's several minutes before either of us speaks.

"Did we move the journals?" she asks weakly.

I glance at the table. They're safe.

"They're utterly destroyed," I tease.

"Liar."

I grin into her neck.

"Then it's me who's destroyed," I tell her earnestly.

She hums, then goes quiet, her hand tracing lazy patterns on my chest.

"I want to see it all," she says softly. "The future. The past. Everything that came before me and everything that might come after."

"You will," I tell her. "You're the queen of all time now."

She tilts her head up to meet my gaze. "Then stay by my side," she says.

"Always," I whisper, kissing her forehead. "Until time itself forgets our names."

LEGACY

EPILOGUE

I slip away from the banquet hall the moment I'm sure no one is paying attention to me. The golden goblets and endless flutes of harp music were giving me a headache anyway. Too many ministers speaking in too many languages, all congratulating each other on another year of peace. I know I should care. It's what's expected of a future queen, but all I could think about was getting out. Out of the tight-laced gown, out of the smiles I've been practicing since I was five.

Out of the noise.

The hallways are cooler now, quiet in the way the castle only is at night. I don't light a torch. I know the way by heart, past the atrium of blooming moonpetals, through the corridor of Starsong glass, until I reach the place that calls me like a whispered promise.

The Royal Gallery.

The guards don't stop me. They know who I am. They only nod, pressing fists to chests, and swing the great silver doors open without a word.

The gallery is dark save for the enchanted sconces lining the walls, each one glowing faintly beside a framed portrait. Not all of them are paintings. Some are carved in marble or etched in glass. Some move. Some sing.

All of them watch.

I walk slowly, heels clicking softly on polished stone as I pass generations of Altinnian rulers. My ancestors. My bloodline. And yet, even now, there's only one I've come here to see.

The farthest wall holds five portraits, larger than life, mounted side by side beneath an arch woven with magic itself.

I don't even look at the others. Not yet. I stop in front of the first, the center.

Queen Maerilee, Queen of All Time.

She doesn't smile in her portrait, but she doesn't need to. Her silver eyes burn through the canvas as if she sees everything, even now. Her hair is braided in the style of warriors long past, her crown light and elegant on her brow. Her wings, luminescent and arched high, glow faintly with the remnants of old magic. She's the only one who doesn't seem like a portrait. She seems alive.

I wrap my arms around myself, exhaling slowly as the magic hums in the back of my mind. I've felt it here before, but tonight is different. There's a charge in the air. A pressure. Like someone's holding their breath.

I lean forward and whisper, "I had to get away."

My voice sounds so small, so young. I'm only sixteen, but that doesn't matter. I could be called upon to be queen at any time, especially if something happens to my mother. Though, unlike Queen Maerilee's mother, Queen Kimalissa, I don't expect anyone would attack mine. We've had peace in Altinna for thousands of years, ever since Queen Maerilee erected the barrier.

"I know I'm supposed to care about all of it, the treaties and the symbolism of it all, but I just don't. Not yet, anyway. I find it horrifically boring."

My fingers twitch at my sides, almost nervously, which is strange, considering I'm speaking to a portrait. I'm sure the guards aren't listening. They're trained not to.

"You didn't start out as Queen of All Time, did you? You were just a girl. Like me."

I press a hand to the cool stone beneath her portrait. And I swear, for a heartbeat, the warmth of another hand presses back.

Everyone knows the story. Even the smallest child in Altinna can recite it.

Queen Maerilee. She was the unbound heir of a faltering kingdom. Her mother, Queen Kimalissa, grew too weak to sustain the barrier. A trusted advisor poisoned her, and Maerilee was the only one who could save the kingdom.

But Maerilee wasn't strong enough on her own. She couldn't access her powers until she found her One. Instead, she found Four.

They came from the corners of a fractured realm. There was the warrior, who'd been protecting her since she was a child. There was the crown prince of a warring kingdom. Most scandalously, was his brother, who'd been raised as a spare, but quickly became one of the most trusted generals in the entire realm. And finally, there was the seer, the man who saw it all coming. She bound herself to them, loved them, fought with them. And with them, she saved our kingdom from collapse.

They say she stood alone on the battlefield when the last of the enemies fell, her body bathed in light, her arms outstretched, the land itself rising to meet her. They say her barrier wasn't built with magic alone but with sacrifice and unity and love.

I finally look at the other four pictures surrounding Maerilee's.

Akin the Strong.

River the Kind.

Brook the Brave.

Permiton the Wise.

The five of them ruled for centuries. And when the day came that one of them faltered–no one knows who passed first–they all followed, one by one. Or maybe they all died together at exactly the same time. No one knows for sure.

Legend has it that their wings were found folded together, that the light never left the room where they lay, and if you go there now, there's still a faint shimmer of light that lingers, even in the dark. Some say they transcended. Others say they simply died like the rest of us.

I, personally, think they're still alive. It's a secret I've never shared with anyone, but I swear I feel them in the castle. Of course, that's what you get when you live in such an ancient place. We have more ghosts than living fae.

To Maerilee's left is River. His hand rests on the hilt of a sword, but his eyes are soft. A smirk hides at the corners of his mouth, like he's just told a joke and is waiting to see if you'll catch it. His parents declared war on Altinna when he and his brother chose to be bound to Maerilee. Because of it, Oceana declared war on Altinna. They say he was vain at first. Cruel, even, but he changed. Maerilee changed him.

Next to him is Brook. He isn't particularly regal or stern like most of the kings in this gallery. He's still and calm. His painting was one of the last completed, after all the wars were over. He stands barefoot in a garden, water swirling around his fingertips. His smile is small, his expression private. The stories say he was gentle, until he wasn't, that he was quiet until the moment demanded more. I like to think I have a little of him in me.

To Maerilee's right is Permiton. They say his mind never stopped turning, that he saw not only the future, but the heart of people. His portrait is done in gold etching, magic woven into the threads of his robe, his hands glowing faintly with Sight, though legends say he actually learned how to travel in time. If that's true, I wish he would come visit me and tell me what to do.

Finally, there's Akin. All accounts say that he died in the first battle of The Great War, but he somehow returned from death. His painting shows him in full armor, scars trailing his arms like stories. His eyes are fierce, but the faint smile at the corners of his mouth tells you he loved just as fiercely as he fought.

I step back and look at all five of them together. They're my family, my ancestors, impossible, extraordinary, and beautiful.

I've always come in here to gaze at their portraits, and felt like I wasn't enough, like I was just a leaf on the great tree of Altinna's history, a flicker of light in the wake of legends.

What am I compared to them?

I don't have wings. I don't speak to the dead. I can barely maintain my shielding magic, and I've never felt called to lead the way my tutors insist I should. I've never been in love, never even wanted to find my One, much less believed I could find Four.

But then again, Maerilee didn't believe either. At least, not at first. She had to fight her fear. Her self-doubt. Her grief. And she did it. So maybe I can too.

I don't realize I'm crying until the warmth on my cheek cools in the air.

I press my fingers beneath my eyes, annoyed. I came here to breathe, not break down like a child. But I don't feel ashamed. I feel suddenly at peace, like someone is wrapping me in a comforting hug.

"Maerilee?" I whisper, just to say it. "Are you here?"

No answer, just the flicker of the sconces, the faint pulse of the portrait's magic. I smile through the ache in my chest.

"I'll be better tomorrow. I promise."

I take one last look at her face, then I turn away. I again feel a presence, a warmth behind me. Like sunlight on the back of my neck. The sense of someone ancient, someone powerful, someone who has always been watching and just now decided to show themselves.

I spin, but there's no one there. Still, my heart hammers in my chest. I know I'm not alone.

Not really. One day, when I really need Queen Maerilee, she'll reveal herself to me. I don't believe much, but I believe that.

I press a hand to my stomach to steady myself and exhale.

"Thank you," I whisper.

The warmth lingers for another heartbeat, then fades. When I return to the banquet, no one questions my absence. They're still drinking, still laughing, still toasting the peace Maerilee won for us.

But I feel different, somehow lighter and heavier at the same time.

One day, I will lead. Maybe not like her. Maybe not as powerful, or as unforgettable. But I will stand where she stood, and I will be ready. Because she's guiding me.

Her story isn't over, and neither is mine.

ALSO BY SADIE WATERS

Chosen by the Princess: A Reverse Harem Romance,

Realm of the Chosen Book 1

Loved by the Princess: A Reverse Harem Romance,

Realm of the Chosen Book 2

Ruled by the Princess: A Reverse Harem Romance,

Realm of the Chosen Book 3

Realm of the Chosen: The Complete Series

Demon Seer: Ember's Flames Book 1

Demon Hunter: Ember's Flames Book 2

Demon Slayer: Ember's Flames Book 3

Queen of Winter

A Sketch Away from Perfect: The Art of Having it All Book 1

A Palette Full of Lovers: The Art of Having it All Book 2

Book Three coming soon!

The One: Four Fae for the Princess Book 1

The Quest: Four Fae for the Princess Book 2

The Crown: Four Fae for the Princess Book 3

Follow me on social media!

Instagram: https://www.instagram.com/sadiewaters/

Facebook: https://www.facebook.com/sadiewatersauthor

Twitter: https://twitter.com/SadieWatersBook

Bookbub: https://www.bookbub.com/authors/sadie-waters

9 798898 710095